Johnny Kellock
Died Today

Johnny Kellock
Died Today

Hadley Dyer

HarperTrophyCanada™
An imprint of HarperCollinsPublishersLtd

Johnny Kellock Died Today
© 2006 by Hadley Dyer.
All rights reserved.

Published by HarperTrophyCanada™,
an imprint of HarperCollins Publishers Ltd

First Edition

HarperTrophyCanada™ is a trademark of
HarperCollins Publishers

HarperCollins books may be purchased for
educational, business, or sales promotional
use through our Special Markets Department.

HarperCollins Publishers Ltd
2 Bloor Street East, 20th Floor
Toronto, Ontario, Canada
M4W 1A8

www.harpercollins.ca

Library and Archives Canada Cataloguing
in Publication

Dyer, Hadley

Johnny Kellock died today / Hadley Dyer.
—1st ed.

ISBN-13: 978-0-00-639533-1
ISBN-10: 0-00-639533-3

I. Title.

PS8607.Y37J63 2006   JC813'.6
C2005-905536-7

RRD 9 8 7 6 5 4

Printed and bound in the United States
Text design by Sharon Kish
Set in Joanna

For my family,
and in memory of Lily and Eisan

Prologue

Johnny Kellock disappeared on August 1, 1959. Or, at least, that's the day after the last day anybody ever saw him.

The rest of the world was lined up on Barrington Street, trying to get a glimpse of Queen Elizabeth and her husband, Prince Philip, on their first trip to Halifax. The Queen wore a pink dress and a white hat, and she looked a lot like television pictures of the Queen but in colour.

Meanwhile, my cousin was disappearing.

Whoosh. Poof. Gone.

No one knew why exactly Johnny did what he did. It's like if you pulled on a bit of yarn, and you pulled and pulled until the whole sweater's come unravelled and you've got a mess of yarn at your feet and then someone has the bright idea that you should try to find the end you started with.

Anyway, as Mama says, a person should stick to their own story. Mine starts when Johnny had already disappeared. And it ends with us Normans doing what we always used to do whenever something bad happened. Or something good. Or every Sunday afternoon if nothing'd happened in between. We gathered round Mama's kitchen table in the usual order, oldest to youngest—Freddie, Margaret, Doris, Young Lil, Martha, and me, Rosalie—and we smoked.

It was my twelfth birthday, and it was my first and only cigarette.

And it was the last time we all sat together like that.

Chapter One

I was sitting on the stairs in our old house on Agricola Street, the backs of my legs sticking to the tiny ridges of the rubber treads. I was working on Norman's face. In the photograph, his eyes were in the shadow of his cap. He was standing beside a cow with a dog in his arms. I had them sketched out already. They stared back, vacant-like, edges fading into the paper. I could fix that. But the thing about it is, when you're drawing your father, the first person you ever saw when you were shooting out into this world, you want to get it right.

See, drawing works in layers. First you sketch out what you're working on—an old picture of Norman, in this case. You stroke the paper, so gentle. Then you add lines and press harder. The drawing gets darker and deeper. The picture starts to sharpen. It becomes real. And you get inside it. You see the crusty snow under your own feet. Wind pushing over frozen fields. A scratchy, woollen hunter's cap. Frost clinging to the tip of a long, perfectly straight nose. You say:

Hey, Norman.

Hello, my Bean.

How much you got?

You know.

How much?

Two cents. One to take the ferry to my mother's on Sunday—

And one to get you back.

"Rosalie Evelyn Norman!"

I looked through the banister rungs at the hard, white surface of the kitchen door. If Mama came through it, she'd know I was on the stairs instead of outdoors. Then she'd see Norman's photograph and her mouth would get stitched up tight. Sure as the roof belonged on the top of the house, the family photos belonged on the wall above the landing, always and forever, two steps up and twelve steps down. I set my pencils and sketch pad on the stairs and returned the picture to its hook. It was hot, and I was in no mood for Mama's mouth.

You probably never heard that I got the oldest mother in the whole world. She was born in 1899. Norman's old, too, but he was born in 1901. Mama's from the last century. She was coming up on fifty when I came along. I tell people that's a world record. The truth is I never looked it up. Having a mother who holds a world record, that's better than having a mother who's just really old.

Mama had been in a foul mood all morning. Usually she just had one mood—and one expression, pinched-like—but I could tell today's was truly foul because she was being quiet. At breakfast, I put two spoonfuls of sugar on my porridge. White sugar from the bowl. Mama didn't even look up from the sink, where she was attacking the potatoes for Sunday's stew. I ended up pushing the sticky porridge around with my spoon because it was too sweet and it got hard and crusty at the edge of the bowl and my forehead was already prickled with sweat.

Just about the only thing Mama'd said that day was when she handed Norman his lunch pail. She said, "I suppose you checked the mail yesterday."

Now, my father always checks the mail—the box is right at the end of our walk. He has never not checked the mail, not for as long as I've been alive. Just like he's never not come into my room at bedtime to sit at the end of my bed and say: "Bean." Just like that. "Bean." Which is like an "open sesame" that makes the whole day come spilling out of my mouth, no matter how sleepy I am or how tired Norman's eyes look.

I might have pointed that out to Mama.

Norman just said: "Yup."

In the summertime, the only thing Mama let you do indoors was chores. If you weren't doing chores you had to go outdoors. You could just stand there like a statue and that was doing something because you were outdoors. But a person indoors, drawing where it's cooler and the pencil doesn't smear from your sweaty hand, that person was doing nothing.

I tiptoed down from the landing and took giant, soft steps across the living room, as if the floor was lake water and I was crossing on lily pads. I eased the screen door shut behind me. You had to lift it by the handle, just so, or it creaked.

The thick air and street noise were like a blast from the warming hub of the stove. The hot porch bit at my feet through my sandals. My blouse wilted against my skin. Our next-door neighbour, Mrs. Hewitt, was working in her flower bed. Her big old rump was tipped up, rising over the hedge like a rhinoceros in a polka-dot bathing cap. Across the street, the Gravedigger was standing on his front stoop.

He wore a heavy plaid shirt and work boots even though the air was so heavy it felt like you could take a bite out of it. His real name was David Flynn, but everybody called him the Gravedigger. He got his nickname because he had a job tending the plots at Fairview Lawn Cemetery. His family had moved into the old Greenwood house a year ago, and when he felt like it, he went to St. Stephen's, the Catholic school.

6

St. Stephen's was next door to my old school, Mulgrave Park. The schools had one yard divided down the middle by a chain-link fence, but we never needed the fence. The Protestants called the Catholic kids "Micks" and the Micks stuck together like rosary beads. They used to shout at us, "Catholics, Catholics, ring the bell! Protestants, Protestants, go to——!" Course, we'd reverse it and shout it right back to them.

That fall, I was going into grade seven at Richmond School, and the Gravedigger, if he'd passed, would be going to Alexander McKay. The junior highs had Fort Needham between them, and that was still too close for me. Take now, for instance. The Gravedigger, standing there on his stoop, seemed to be staring straight at our house. Zombie-like. There was no further word from Mama—aw, she was just making sure I was outdoors—so it seemed like maybe this was a good time to mosey over to Millner's Corner Store, see if anyone was getting a Popsicle.

Up the street, little kids were playing jump rope, kick-the-can, jacks. You always play jacks with your back to the east. If you play with your back to the west and your ball bounces away from you, there's a better chance it'll start rolling. See, Agricola runs through the North End along the hill coming down from the water reservoir. The houses on the west side, where the Gravedigger lives, are up higher up on the hill than on the east side, where I live. Farther east, the ground slopes up again to Fort Needham and then back down to the shipyard. If you went to the northernest part of the North End—which you wouldn't, because you don't have no reason to—eventually you'd get to Africville, where a lot of the black people live, and if you kept on going, you'd fall into the harbour. If you headed south past the Hydrostone Market—which you wouldn't, because Mama would tear your eyebrows off if you went farther than Young Street without asking—you'd be on your way to the South End, where the rich people live. There's another hill, a big one, Citadel Hill, between the rich people and the regular people, and don't tell me that wasn't on purpose.

The bench outside of Millner's was empty. You could tell no one had been on it for a while because it burned the back of my legs when I tried to sit down. Most of the kids my age would be swimming down at the Northwest Arm or Chocolate Lake on a day like today. I didn't like swimming. You couldn't see without your glasses. Your foot was always brushing against something slimy. Also, it was no fun when your best friend, Marcy, was spending the summer with cousins in Pugwash and wasn't there to keep the boys from splashing and pulling you under. It wasn't easy being with the girls, either, not without Marcy, not since Nan Buckler made fun of me for saying *tomawto* instead of *tomayto*. People kept on about it, too, when they should've taken my side. Everybody knows the Bucklers are common enough to reuse their teabags.

That's why I'd spent half the summer sneaking indoors and being ordered right back out again. That's why I was so bored, I started counting the number of steps from Millner's back to my house. When I was done counting the steps, I would probably count the hairs on my arms. And then the number of seconds in the two weeks and twenty-one hours before I officially turned twelve, which wasn't anything to look forward to since my best friend was going to miss it by a day. And since we're counting, that's how I came to know that there are 198 steps between Millner's and where I stepped into the Gravedigger's shadow.

He was standing on the street in front of our house. I was on the sidewalk and he was down on the street, and I still had to tilt my head back to look at him. His head blocked out the sun.

"Been held back once already," Marcy had said last fall. "He's the biggest kid in the history of the sixth grade." We were at the classroom window, watching the Gravedigger leave the school-yard in the middle of the afternoon. "Can you imagine working in the same graveyard where your own mother is buried?" Marcy grabbed my arm. "Rosalie! I wonder if he ever dug her up!" Now, I knew that was ridiculous. Even so, when the rumour went around that the Gravedigger *had* dug up his mother and kept her body in a jelly cupboard, I stopped walking on the Flynns' side of the street.

"You one of the Norman girls?" the Gravedigger asked. I nodded. "I got something for Fred Norman." He stepped up on the sidewalk and took a letter out of his back pocket.

The sun was pounding on my shoulders, heating up my dark hair. I'd never been so close to the Gravedigger. It was kind of like seeing the Queen coming out of Government House a couple of weeks before. I mean, you're looking at a person, and you're supposed to be thinking, "God bless her royal personage" or "I'll scream if he touches me." But at the same time you're kind of distracted, comparing what the person looks like to what you always thought they looked like. The Gravedigger's eyes aren't black, as you might expect. They're green-blue with shadowy edges, and they have a way of getting greener and meaner when they're staring down at you.

"Fred Norman? Freddie lives in Dartmouth."

"You sure?" The Gravedigger looked down at the envelope, wiping the sweat away from his eyes with his sleeve. His hair was black and damp against his forehead. "Says Mr. and Mrs. Frederick Norman. Come from Ship Harbour."

"Sure I'm sure. He's my brother, isn't he? He and his wife live at 86 Cherry Street in Dartmouth. But you can leave it with me."

"Maybe it's for Fred Senior, then."

"Who?"

Mrs. Hewitt popped up from behind the hedge. She had something to say about everything, and everything she said was so important, she had to say it twice. Somehow it always sounded like she was accusing you of something.

"Young man, you well know that I'm a trusted neighbour. I tell you, I'm a trusted neighbour." She pointed at the Gravedigger with the trowel in her pudgy hand. "What's this about?"

"Look, I got a letter here," the Gravedigger said. "It went to our house by mistake. Alls I care about is getting it to Fred Norman, like my dad asked, or I'm gonna catch it. She's telling me he don't live here."

"Rosa-lee!" That's another thing about Mrs. Hewitt. She says my name like two names and neither of them nice. "Rosa-lee! It's for your father!"

Norman.

I straightened up, Mama-like, and held out my hand. The Gravedigger's dirty fingers left a brown smear on the envelope. He turned and crossed the street and didn't look back.

"Rosa-lee!" said Mrs. Hewitt. "What did you think your father's name was?"

I was looking at the space the Gravedigger left behind. "Norman."

"That's your surname. What did you think his first name was?"

"Nor—" I caught myself. Too late.

"Norman Norman? What kind of a name is that?" She howled, throwing up her hands.

"I—I don't know."

In comic books, when a character has a major revelation, the background goes all swirly. Then you get up close to the person's eyes and their whole world is swimming around in there. You don't need words, not even a thought bubble, to know what the person is saying in their head:

How is it even halfway possible this didn't sink in before?

"Thank goodness I was here. Let's get this letter to your poor mother. Lily! There's a letter come, dear! I say, there's a—"

The noise from inside the house sounded almost like Mama had let go of an armload of books. Then, like an echo, came a moan, and then, under it, the sound of something dropping. From one surface to another with a pitter-pat-pat-pat. I felt the blood drain from my face, just like they say in novels, only I didn't think on it as I ran up the steps towards the house.

Inside, Mama was lying on the stairs with her leg twisted behind her. My pencils, rolling along our old sloped floors, met me at the door.

Chapter Two

"By God," said Mrs. Hewitt when she saw Mama on the stairs. "The mighty has fallen." Mama looked up into her pudding face. "Are you all right, Lillian? I say, are you all right? What are we doing here?"

Mama's mouth drew together in a tight line. I stepped back a bit. You'd think that, having lived in a port city through a couple of wars, Mrs. Hewitt would know a thing or two about shrapnel, but she was leaning in close when Mama fired. "I'm lying on the damn stairs, Mag! What in God's name does it look like I'm doing!"

When Norman pulled up in the Nelson Seed truck twenty minutes later, Mrs. Hewitt had managed to help Mama sit up. Mama was still spitting curse words at her like a machine gun.

"Lily," he said, when he saw the bruise spreading down the side of her face.

"Just a bump," she cut him off. "I told Mag not to bother you at work."

"Hush that. No one was using the truck. We'll go to the hospital."

Before she could say another word, Norman lifted Mama into his arms and carried her out to the car as easily as though she were a sack of seed.

Norman was old, but he was strong. That's because he had about a hundred brothers and sisters. By the time he was my age, they slept stacked on top of each other like fish fillets. So Norman was sent off to work at his cousin's farm. They paid him two cents a week. One to take the ferry to his mother's on Sunday and, well, you know the rest.

"It's probably just a sprain," Norman said, when he came back for Mama's purse. "And the shock of it. They'll fix her up."

I watched the truck until it turned off Agricola Street. The pencils were everywhere, tucked against baseboards and under mats. As I gathered them up, their painted wood hummed in my hands.

The house was quiet.

Back when everyone still lived under the same roof, there was never a quiet time. Margaret and Doris shared one bedroom, and Young Lil, Martha, and me shared another. Freddie's bed was the chesterfield. He kept his clothes in a wardrobe in the hallway. There were always kids coming and going, always bodies around the kitchen table, drinking tea from the pot simmering on the back of the stove, smoking, bickering, aggravating Mama, teasing Norman.

Everything had pretty much happened by the time I came along. I knew the stories by heart. I could play like a reel the time Freddie threw his shoe at Mama, joking-like, after she beat him at rummy, and she ducked and it smashed through the kitchen window, and I thought, "He's going to die." Wait, I was alive for that one. Mama laughed and we all just about cried with the relief of it. But I can also see, clear as day, the explosion up at Magazine Hill shaking the house and a piece of ceiling falling into my sister Doris's birthday cake as she was leaning over to blow out the candles—and that was two years before I was even born.

I suppose there was a time when Mama's hair wasn't white and her hands weren't spotted. I don't remember it. Ever since I was little, when I kissed Mama's cheek, her skin was as soft and wrinkled as tissue paper. Mama wasn't kissy anyway, not like other mothers. She wasn't at all like other mothers. For instance, a person should be allowed to sneeze at the dinner table. If you sneeze at the dinner table, a mother should say: "Bless you." My mother said: "Stop it."

Other mothers wore dresses, not housedresses and aprons. Other mothers wore lipstick and went to church on Sunday.

15

Other mothers let you drink tea with lots of milk and sugar. Not the World's Oldest Mother. And I'd sent her to the hospital.

"That'll do," Mrs. Hewitt said to the boiled chicken she was prodding. "Rosa-lee, dear. You'll be turning off those beans in three minutes—three minutes, no more. Or they'll be the soft-as-mush variety of your mother's."

That was it for me, I have to say. It was one thing for Mrs. Hewitt to laugh at my foolishness. But she must not stand in this house and insult Mama's cooking or anything else. Not tonight.

"Mrs. Hewitt." My voice was tight and high. "Thank you for helping me with Mama, but . . ."

I felt around for the words.

"But what, dear?"

"But . . ." But I could only manage, "I like soft-as-mush beans."

"Course you do, dear. Course you do. By God, it's what you're accustomed to. You say you'll be all right until Martha gets home? Right, then. I've got to find Mr. Hewitt and get his supper on."

I knew where Mr. Hewitt was. He was hiding from Mrs. Hewitt. The Hewitts had a perfectly good front porch that Mrs. Hewitt washed down with a hose every day, even though the only people who were ever on it were her cats, and strictly

16

speaking, cats aren't people. But anyone who ever spent any time with Mrs. Hewitt wouldn't need to ask why Mr. Hewitt didn't sit on his own porch. One time I spotted him reading a book in a tree in their backyard while she was going up and down the street calling for him.

Martha phoned from the library to say she was meeting Norman at the hospital and had I eaten and had I remembered to put the leftovers in the refrigerator and would I be okay? I didn't say anything about the pencils. It would be just like Martha to think that paying for them somehow made her responsible for Mama's fall. Like how she'd apologize to my sisters when their smoking bothered her asthma. She bought most of my art supplies out of her paycheque from the library, which she was supposed to be saving for university next year. Martha's the smartest, gentlest person ever—even more than Norman, truthfully. She's got hands that are as pale and soft as milk even when she's stuffing me into my Sunday clothes. Norman's are like mattresses—a little rough on the surface but so big and cushy you feel like you could curl up on his palm like Thumbelina. The closest Martha gets to being fierce is when she's correcting my talking or getting after me about rotting my brain with comics. Norman, on the other hand, gets fierce enough to shoot at Mrs. Hewitt's cats from the back step with a BB-gun when they tear around our garden.

I got ready for bed as the sun was going down. Through my bedroom window, I saw the Gravedigger shuffling down his walk, carrying an old lantern. A little shudder went up my spine. People had seen mysterious lights in the cemetery at night, swooping up among the treetops. They said that later, if you had guts enough to stick around, you'd see the Grave-digger leaving the grounds with a lantern in his hand.

I grabbed my sketch pad and the shoebox where I kept my art supplies and sat down at the window with my bum on a big cardboard box. At the end of the school year, Freddie and his wife, Hazel, had brought a big stack of comic books over in the box. Real old stuff. There was a bunch in this series called *Tales of Terror* that's now banned. Martha says that's because the gov-ernment thinks horror comics make you right delinquent. For example, you might read a story about a butcher's wife who cuts up her husband's body to sell to his customers, and then go out and murder somebody. The only thing comics ever made me was mad that I can't buy the Sea Monkeys and other good stuff they advertise at the back. You can't get them anywhere around here. You have to mail a money order to Yahookaville, U.S.A.

I opened my sketch pad to a fresh page. First I drew a block of squares. Inside the first square, I drew the Gravedigger hold-ing his lantern, little smell-waves coming off him. In a box above his head, I wrote: "*Motherless! Godless! Abandoned and feared by all!!"* In the next square, I drew an old hag. Introductions to scary comics always have an old hag. Warty pickle nose. Frizzled hair. Spit dripping from her teeth. Truth be told, this one looked a lot like my late Great-aunt Mavis. In a big speech bubble I wrote:

WELCOME, *VERMIN!* IF YOU WILL *VENTURE* INTO THE *TOMB OF TERROR*, YOUR HOST, *THE TOMB-KEEPER*, WILL *TELL* YOU A *TALE*. I HAVE SELECTED A *DEADLY SERIOUS STORY*. AND I DO MEAN **DEADLY!** SO CURL UP IN YOUR *COFFINS*, AND I'LL BEGIN MY *TERRIBLE TALE* CALLED . . . *THE GRAVEDIGGER COMETH!!!*

That's when I remembered I was home by myself for the first time ever.

I'm not saying I was scared exactly, but sometimes a person likes to have all the lights on in the house. I went around and put them on, kind of humming to myself, you know how you do. I peered into Mama and Norman's bedroom. I almost never went in there and I'd never, ever touched anything—ever. Young Lil once took an old silk handkerchief from Mama's dresser, and when Mama found out it was like the other explosion, the big one in the harbour, back in 1917. The Great Disaster. Practically blew the North End off the map. The new

Richmond School was said to be haunted by the ghost of a little girl who was still searching for the other eighty-eight kids who never made it to the old Richmond School that morning. Course, I was sorry to have reminded myself about that one.

Norman had a bowl of candies on his bedside table and Mama had a big jar of Noxema on hers. Mama used Noxema for everything. She washed her face with it, rubbed it on my sunburns and Norman's callused hands. Beside the jar of Noxema was a turquoise telephone, heavy and squat like a big blue frog. We were one of the only families in the North End that had a private line, let alone a second phone, let alone a fancy blue phone *upstairs.* The wiring had been paid for by the great-aunties, who'd raised Mama and were bedridden for years before they died. Uncle Jim once told me the new upstairs phone caused quite a stir in the neighbourhood and it was the excitement of it, not the flu, that killed the great-aunties shortly after, which made it a right smart investment to his mind, and Mama said, "I did not hear that, Jim." I don't know why we kept the phone, since Mama hardly seemed to use it.

I stepped one toe into the room.

Rrrrring!

The blue frog went off like an alarm and my heart smacked hard against my ribs. It was three, four rings before my organs went back to their natural order and I got my whole self into the room.

"Hello? . . . Hello?"

Silence. And then a dial tone.

Now, in comic books, when they want to skip ahead a bit, they just show a couple of panels without words. If I were drawing the story of my life, this is what it'd look like:

Me with my eyeballs popping out.

My bare feet running across the hall.

Me in bed with the covers pulled up, little old hags reflected in my eyeballs.

The hands on our grandfather clock spinning.

When Norman came into my room, I was asleep with my cheek on *A Child's Illustrated Bible Stories*.

"Norman?"

"You fell asleep with all the lights on."

"Where's everybody?"

"In bed."

"Did Mama have an X-ray?"

"Yup."

"Will she have to wear a cast?"

"Yup."

"Is her leg broken?"

"Doctor says the ankle's fractured."

"Is she—is she going to be okay?"

"Looks like. Don't expect she'll be up for family tomorrow."

Norman's gaze drifted towards the shoebox on my window sill. He didn't need to say a word for me to know that he'd seen the pencils on the floor when he came for Mama. For the first time since then, the tears spilled over. They ran down my face and neck and until the collar of my nightgown was soaked.

"Where'd that come from?" he said finally. He reached over to my nightstand and picked up the letter the Gravedigger had brought over.

"It went across the street by mistake. Norman?"

"Bean."

"How come everybody calls you Norman?"

I couldn't look my father in the face, so I kept my eyes on the edge of his grey pants, stark against the yellow sheets Mama had ironed just that morning.

"I suppose it was Jim who started it, calling us farmhands by our last names. You know, MacDonald, Kellock, Norman. And your brother always had to do like your Uncle Jim. Then Margaret picked it up. Let's see . . . There's a story about names and Jim from way back when."

"What happened?"

"This is before Jim introduced me to your mother, so I'm telling it second-hand, right?"

"Okay."

"Okay, story goes that Mama and Aunt Izzie used to spend summers at Friar's Lake. Sometimes your uncle went out, too, when he could get off the farm. One day a young feller named Marshall Briggsby comes running up the path yelling, 'Jimmy's drowning! Jimmy's drowning!' Course, Mama and your Aunt Izzie go tearin' down to the lake, thinking their brother's out there in the water. Then they hear people laughing. There's old Marshall and his pals having a good one. A joke, see?

"So, a few weeks later your Uncle Jim's down for another visit when who comes up the path but Marshall Briggsby. He's huffing and puffing and he starts in, 'Jimmy's drowning! Jimmy's drowning!'

"And your Mama, she says, 'See here, Marshall, I know darn well my Jimmy is sitting in the cottage drinking the Coke Cola I poured him m'self. So you'd better keep on running.'

"Seeing's how he wasn't getting far with the Duchess—er, that's what people called her sometimes—Marshall hightailed it for the next cottage."

"Uncle Jim was inside, wasn't he?"

"Yes, Bean, he was. But young Jimmy MacPherson from Prospect was in the water, and he died."

"But Mama didn't know it was a different Jimmy," I cried. "Marshall didn't explain, and anyway it's his own fault for telling lies . . ."

"I figure it don't matter how small a mistake starts out," said Norman. "You have to live with it all the same." The hand on my foot was heavy and warm through the sheets. "Just ask your Mama."

Norman's eyes were tired. And suddenly, even though my mind was filled up with poor old dead Jim MacPherson from Prospect and how I didn't know my own father's name and how I almost killed my mother, it came into my head how to fix Norman's portrait.

The tick-tick of the grandfather clock climbed the stairs from the landing. I crawled out from under the sheets and kissed my father's scratchy salt-and-pepper cheek. "Thanks, Papa," I said, using my old baby name for him.

"Frederick Floyd Norman," he said, holding out a peat-stained hand. "Pleased to make your acquaintance."

Chapter Three

The next morning, Sunday, I found Mama sitting up in bed wearing a fresh housedress and reading a Louis Lamour novel. Her hair was braided and neatly pinned, like always. She looked for all the world as though she'd just sat down for a moment, except for the plaster cast that covered her leg halfway up to the knee and the dark bruise raised on her face. The cast was propped up on a pillow. I'd never seen Mama in her bed before.

The blue frog looked at me accusingly.

"Martha's getting breakfast on," Mama said. "Your father told Mag Hewitt we don't need help today, so don't you go letting her in." She didn't look up from her book.

When I'd woken up, my chest felt squeezed and tight, as though my ribs had become a size too small. Now it was like someone had let the air out of me. Was it possible that Mama didn't know about the pencils on the stairs? She'd seemed so lost after her fall. Could it be that she didn't realize it was my fault? And no one had told her?

Downstairs, Martha was flushed as she stirred the oatmeal, though the kitchen was early-morning cool. "Norman called Aunt Izzie this morning," she said. "He's going to keep the truck an extra day so he can bring her that old wardrobe. Do you want raisins?"

My feet slapped across the linoleum. "Yup, yup, yup."

"I wouldn't be surprised if he brought Aunt Izzie back with him."

"Can't remember the last time she was here," I said. "But I bet Norman wouldn't drive two hours to Ship Harbour if he didn't hope he could talk her into coming."

Martha set my bowl in front of me and swiped the comic book I'd propped against the milk bottle off the table. "You know, a while back Mama said that Aunt Izzie got all worked up because Johnny wanted to come to Halifax and get a job at the shipyard," she said. "I don't like the idea of him dropping out of school either, but it would be nice if they both ended up here."

I leaned over the oatmeal and felt the steam break like a wave across my face. "I think you're thinking having Johnny around would really shake things up."

I liked the way that sounded when it came out of me. People aren't always straight when they talk, especially when they're talking to the youngest. Even Martha sometimes put on a coat of sugar on things.

Martha tapped me on the head with a knuckle. "I mean, wouldn't it work out nicely for everyone if we had the company, not to mention some help."

The thing about sugar is, it's real hard to scrape off.

The last time Johnny came into the city was for Young Lil's wedding, two summers ago. Uncle Ezra and Aunt Izzie didn't come because one or the other of them wasn't feeling well. Let me tell you, after Cousin Johnny pulled up in his father's car, girls from all over the North End were suddenly going crazy with errands on Agricola Street. You never seen so much traffic back and forth in front of the house. That's because Johnny had grown into what you'd call a tall drink of water. He was fifteen, then, same as Martha. He had night-black hair, like Mama's in old pictures, and her blue eyes, too, not brown like the rest of us. Mostly I liked the easy way about him. He listened closely and laughed at near anything you said.

Once, when I was small, I told him, "I'm going to marry you when I grow up." Martha's cheeks turned pink, and I quickly added, "After you marry Martha." Which only made her go from pink to red.

Johnny laughed. "People don't get that lucky twice."

After the wedding, the grown-ups headed for the church hall and danced all night. Martha and me were the only ones who made it to church the next morning. On the way out, we stepped over my brother Freddie and my sister Margaret's husband, Cecil. They were sleeping side by side on the floor, each with his arm flung over the other. When we got back, those grown-up Normans were sitting around the kitchen table, holding their heads, smoking. Martha said, "Where's Johnny?"

Everyone started looking around the room as though he was a cat that might have gone behind the stove. That's when Johnny came in through the back door. His hand was gripping his night-black hair like it was dragging him along.

Freddie hollered, "So, you caught the last dance with Sarah Hatfield after all!"

There was a lot of hooting and slapping the table—until we saw Mama bringing up the rear.

"Found this one face down in my dahlias. You'd think, son," Mama said to Freddie, "you'd show your cousin a little more hos-pit-al-ity. At least take the bottle out from under him so he can get a decent night's sleep in your mother's flower bed."

Johnny smoothed down his matted hair. "Sorry, Aunt Lily," he said.

If anyone else in that kitchen had been caught sleeping one off in the garden, they would have been chased from the house with a broom. But Mama had a soft spot for Johnny on account of him being Aunt Izzie's one and only, and she just pulled another stool up to the table. "I'll get breakfast on," she said, heading for the pantry. "I'm ashamed of all of you."

Johnny looked so sheepish that everyone started laughing again.

Norman carried Mama downstairs and got her settled. He leaned his big black umbrella against the chesterfield, in case she needed to move around, and set up the radio so she could listen to a service. My parents almost never went to church. Norman said he didn't need people eavesdropping on his prayers, and Mama said she'd had her religious education, thank you. Truth be told, she didn't go anywhere if she could help it. That didn't get the rest of us out of it, though.

From my bedroom window, I heard Norman talking to someone outside.

"Don't worry about the lawn," he was saying. "I'm more concerned about Mrs. Norman's garden getting weeded."

When I saw who he was talking to, I ran downstairs. Martha was fixing her hat in the hall mirror. She looked from my face to the screen door. "Don't," she whispered. "Don't make a fuss. You know Norman only has one day off and he needs the help. You go be polite."

I stepped out onto the porch. It was hot already and my Sunday clothes were itchy. But I was polite. "Good morning," I said to the Gravedigger, who was standing by himself in the yard. Then, to be extra nice, I added, "Don't blame you for not going to church on a day like this. Not when there's work to be had."

"I'm waiting for Fred Senior," said the Gravedigger. "He still out back getting the clippers? Or is he in Dartmouth today?"

I might not have been so well mannered, I tell you, if Martha hadn't come out just then.

I love church. I love the hollow sound of my heels as I walk up the aisle. I love the dark shiny wood that's like tight, ripe apple skin. I love the women in their Sunday clothes. The smell of powder and perfume. The heavy, felt-lined collection plate. The worn-soft hymn book. First thing I do when I get to church, after I'm done looking at what everyone's wearing, is open the hymn book and feel the paper between my fingers. Delicate as onion peel. I lift a page and pass my hand under the words. Strong words, fierce words, God words. I'm no Baptist, but when I sing hymns, I'm as thunderous and holy as Sunday.

I was still thinking on the Gravedigger when we got to church that morning. About how Norman, who was usually a sensible person, didn't seem worried about leaving Mama at home with a boy who had a fondness for dead bodies. Maybe he would dig a big hole in the yard and then start thinking about how to fill it! I hoped Mrs. Hewitt was planning on coming by, and I don't hope that very often.

The minister asked everyone to stand for the Creation hymn:

Many and great, O God, are your works
O Lord of every shining constellation
Long before time and the earth were begun

When I was singing those words, all my worries about Mama eased up. Martha's voice was soft and deep, deeper than you would expect. I liked the way our voices sounded together and how they fit with the congregation's. Funny how you can listen to the whole congregation, then, if you think about it, you can hear your own voice. Or someone else's, like Martha's. Or just the men, or just the women. Or just that old lady in the pew behind you who must have been in a choir once and still thinks she's God's gift to music because she's really caterwauling and her voice has a phony trill to it so you work even harder to hear yourself.

At the end of the hymn, I felt a tap on my shoulder. It was the caterwauler. She was wearing a skinny ol' dead fox around her neck with the head and tail still attached. "Next time, dear," she said, "maybe you should just mouth the words."

She said more than that, but I didn't hear any of it because I was turned back around in my seat, a hot flush running from my ears down my back. I felt Martha's hand over mine and started trembling all over what with trying to keep the tears from leaking out.

Later, when the collection plate was going around, I could hear the caterwauler whispering to the old bag beside her that she was just trying to be helpful. Because of her voice, you know. Only trying to help. Can't blame a person for helping. Oh yes, only trying to help. Then Martha turned around and gave them some kind of a look.

We walked home with Martha's friends Susan and Amy. Around the back, the Gravedigger was trimming the edges of the lawn. Mama was in the kitchen having tea with Mrs. Hewitt. I felt bad that I'd forgotten to be worried about Mama, and then I was mad at the caterwauler all over again because she made me forget. I went straight upstairs and took out my sketch pad. Before I was even out of my good clothes, the caterwauler was torn apart by a pack of foxes. I don't meant to boast, but the picture was so good, it kind of turned my stomach.

"Rosalie Evelyn Norman!"

If you had told me a few days earlier that I'd be standing on the back step holding a plate with the Gravedigger's lunch on it, I wouldn't have believed you. But there I was, handing him his ham sandwich with a side of potato chips and a glass of milk to wash it down. He just took everything and started eating.

All of a sudden I wasn't scared so much as just peed off at the Gravedigger, sitting there in his work shirt and heavy boots in the middle of summer, like he wanted to be even bigger and sweatier and smellier than he already was. It was his own fault if people didn't like him. And anyway, what was so scary about him? It's not like he went around killing people—he just dug them up. He was a dog of a human being and I wasn't going to be scared of him any more.

"You know, civilized people say thank you," I said.

"Civilized people know their father's proper names."

Dog! Mick! Gravedigger!

"Don't you get too comfortable," I said. "When my cousin Johnny gets here, he can do this stuff and other stuff, too, and then you'll be out of a job."

The Gravedigger took a long drink of milk. He wiped his mouth on his shirtsleeve. "Your cousin's not coming," he said. "He's missing."

Chapter Four

"What do you mean missing?"

"He's run off."

"How do you know?"

The Gravedigger's cheeks were full of sandwich. He swallowed and shrugged. "Didn't you know he was itching to leave?"

Martha *had* mentioned that Johnny wanted to get a job. "You're full of it," I said. "Everybody knows Johnny's been talking about working at the shipyard. But he wouldn't just go off without telling anyone."

"Yeah? Then how come he did?"

"Who says he did?"

"Go ask your parents. Don't got nothing to do with me."

The Gravedigger went back to his sandwich. I could hear Mama and Mrs. Hewitt's voices through the kitchen window.

Well, I wasn't going to ask in front of Mrs. Hewitt. But I made good and sure my foot knocked over the Gravedigger's milk on my way inside. That's what you get for stirring up trouble.

When Norman got home from Ship Harbour at suppertime, he was alone. "Izzie was happy to see that old wardrobe," he said, hanging his hat on the hook. "Garden looks good."

"How's the station?" Mama asked.

"Keeping them all busy."

Keeping them *all* busy.

"Did you see Johnny?" I asked. "We were thinking maybe he and Aunt Izzie would be coming back with you."

"No, he wasn't around. Anyway, Izzie couldn't leave Ezra to run things on his own." He looked over at Mama with his eyebrows making an apology.

Mama shrugged like she wasn't expecting to hear anything different. "When you own the only gas station in the village, you can't just come and go as you like," she said.

"Where was he? Johnny, I mean," I asked.

"Oh, I don't know, Bean. A boy that age doesn't tell his mother everywhere he's going."

That lying Gravedigger, making it sound like Johnny had run away.

Martha was chewing on the inside of her lip like she does when she's worrying about something. "I called everyone to cancel Sunday dinner, like you asked, Mama," she said. "And—and I talked to them about getting a little help around here. Well, you know Margaret's got the young ones to look after, and Freddie lives too far away to be coming by every day. Doris is getting ready for the baby. She says she can't do much in this heat anyway."

"And you'll never peel Young Lil away from that new house," added Mama. "Warms a mother's heart to hear how busy her children are. Yes, it does, sitting here in the house where I birthed them all."

"So unless there's someone else . . ." Martha sighed. "I'll talk to Mrs. Johnson at the library. The other part-time girl is saving for her wedding and says she'll take my shifts."

"You tell Mrs. Johnson you'll give that girl some of your shifts," said Mama. She waved off Martha's look of surprise. "It's not good for a girl your age to be home all the time."

"What will we do around here?"

"Well," said Norman, in his slow way. "This David feller done a good job today. He can help with the yard work. And we'll pitch in around the house, won't we, Bean?"

He gave me a wink, but I was stuck on what he was saying about this David feller.

"The Gravedigger's staying on?"

"What did you call him?"

36

The thing about Norman is, he has a way of dumping shame over a person like a bucket of water.

"Nothing."

"Good. He's a decent young feller and a hard worker."

For Norman, being a hard worker is just about the nicest thing you can say about a person, so I was careful when I said, "He might be good in the garden, but some people would tell you he's a liar. Some people would tell you he's even said lies about this family."

"Since when did you ever listen to anything but the sound of your own voice?" said Mama. "You just mind your own business."

"But Mama, he's a Catholic."

Mama was always telling us not to get tangled up with sailors, Frenchmen, or Micks.

"There's Catholics and there's Catholics. And unless you grow extra arms to do everything that needs doing around here, I'm not going to hear another word about it. But Norman, not on Sunday again."

Norman nodded.

"So it's settled?" asked Martha. "I can keep my job?"

There are some things I think I'll never learn how to draw. Sunshine floating in a glass of water, for one, and Martha's smile.

* * *

I liked to get up early in the summertime. Agricola Street was always quiet, as if noise was colour and had no place in the blue-grey morning light. Norman would be downstairs already, reading the newspaper, his finger following the lines. I'd sit across from him at the kitchen table and have two drawings finished before I was even all the way waked up. Those were my morning exercises. You have to exercise a lot to keep up your drawing muscle. That's what I call the callus on the side of the middle finger on my right hand. If my drawing muscle starts going down, I haven't been exercising enough.

The Gravedigger started coming to our house every day for an hour or two. He cut the grass, weeded Mama's flower garden, worked in the vegetable patch. Sometimes Martha got him to help with heavy chores around the house, like taking down the windows and washing them. Then his arms would be two colours where the soap splashed and cut through the dirt. One time Martha offered to add his clothes to the laundry, but he just shook his head.

It's because I got up so early that I knew the Gravedigger came round the back way, cutting through the McCormacks' yard, which was behind ours. I'd see him through my bedroom window, leaving the house with his father and two brothers. They near took up the whole of Agricola Street, walking side by side in their coveralls and steel-capped boots, swinging their lunch pails. I don't know where the Gravedigger went in the meantime, but as soon as the sun was overhead, he'd show up on the back step.

I stayed clear of the Gravedigger those first few days. For once, I was glad that mostly old people lived on this stretch of Agricola—no other kids my age to look out a window and spot the Gravedigger digging in our yard. Didn't need that following me to junior high in September. But Mama's ankle was going to be in a cast for six weeks, and if my parents kept him on after school started, it was going be hard to keep it quiet.

I knew Marcy would be loyal, but I already had a taste of the other girls' teasing and that was enough. You try always being the second shortest person in the class and having glasses and being told you say "tomato" like a hoity-toity person—no matter what Martha says about you sounding like you were raised in a trashcan—and see if you like the idea of going to a new school where the only thing the older kids know about you is that you have a pal called the Gravedigger. I had to find a way to show my parents that he wasn't fit to have around. And it seemed it had to be worse than him taking a little seed of truth, something small and harmless, and growing it into something big and awful.

Something niggled, though. How did he know Johnny wouldn't be there when Norman went to Ship Harbour? I supposed Aunt

Izzie might have mentioned it when Norman called that morning. And let's say it came up when Norman and Mama, or maybe Mama and Mrs. Hewitt, were talking. And say the Gravedigger overheard them. What made him think he could get away with a lie like that for more than two seconds? Did he imagine I'd run crying to my mother, while he listened at the kitchen window, going "HAHAHAHAHAHAHA!"? That was just plain stupid. Trouble is, I couldn't shake the feeling he was smarter than he looked.

One morning the rain was beating on the windows by the time I finished my morning exercises. I curled up in Norman's old horsehair chair and looked through photo albums. I found one of Mama, Aunt Izzie, and Uncle Jim standing on the porch of our house. 1906. They were wrapped up in winter clothes and huddled together like baby birds. Aunt Izzie was peeking at Mama out of the corner of her eye.

Next came our baby pictures, school pictures, and weddings, starting with my sister Margaret's when I was five. Mama had put me in curlers the day before the wedding and I'd tossed and turned all night with them digging into my scalp. The next morning, Doris and Young Lil pulled the rods from my hair and combed the tangled curls so hard that my head bounced around and I near got seasick. Mama said that once the family portrait was taken I could take my too-tight shoes off until the ceremony, but Uncle Ezra took forever getting it set up. I was wearing a little heart-shaped locket that Margaret gave me because I was the flower girl and I sucked on it hard. Just when my chest felt like it was about to burst open with a big sob, I felt Johnny's hand on my head, the cuff of his jacket among my ringlets. I remember how he pushed a curl away from my ear and whispered, "Wait a minute. Anyone can take anything for a minute."

"Then what?" I whispered back.

He said, "You wait another minute."

I was too little to know how long a minute was, so I started counting all the numbers I knew instead, and before I finished, Uncle Ezra took the picture.

The telephone rang. "Rosalie!" Mama called from upstairs.

"What?!"

"What do you think?"

I got the phone.

"Who is this?" a voice demanded.

Mama would have killed me if I was ever that rude. "It's Rosalie Norman." I lowered my voice. "Who's this?"

"Your Uncle Jim. How's tricks?"

Uncle Jim lived in Toronto. He worked in construction and lived in a neighbourhood full of Greeks and Cape Bretoners. Mama worried about him being far away in the big city, even though Uncle Jim said he always did his best to stay in the easternmost part.

"Hi, Uncle Jim. I'm good."

"Married yet?"

"I'm only eleven!"

"Chinese people marry when they're ten."

The thing about my uncle was, you never knew when he was making stuff up or when he was telling you something true that he just wanted you to think he made up. He also had a glass eye that he liked to pop out and put in your Coke Cola or your pocket, and when you found it and screamed, he'd say, "I got my eye on you, kid."

"Are you calling for Mama? I don't know if she'll come to the phone because her ankle is sort of broken. Did you know that? She has a cast and everything. She fell down the stairs."

"Listen, kid. I don't mean any disrespect to your mother, but there's a lot of good things a person could be doing with her time, and breaking her leg isn't one of them."

"Actually, she fractured her ankle."

"Good, it only cost me three dollars in long distance to clear that up. Now put your mother on."

"I don't know if she'll—"

"Tell her there's two guys named Monstropolis and McAlibi holding their guns to my head."

I ran up to Mama's room, where she was on her bed, rubbing Noxema into her liver spots. She reached for the blue frog and I ran back downstairs to hang up the line. When I picked up the receiver no one was speaking. I waited. And waited.

I yelled up the stairwell, "Mama!"

"Lord lovin'!" Uncle Jim said into my ear. "Lil, hang up and call back on the kid. I can hear her fine from here."

How come adults don't ever want you overhearing even half a sentence?

Later, as I poured myself a Coke Cola, I realized that Uncle Jim knew darn well about Mama's leg, or else why would he call? The only time he ever phoned us long distance was when he couldn't come home for Christmas. He didn't write often, and when he did, his letters were always very short. I'd long ago figured out that they were really just an excuse to get Mama's goat with newspaper articles about armed robberies and axe murders in the big city. Every time a bit of newsprint fell out of a birthday card, Mama's mouth pulled so tight it practically disappeared. Shame of it is, Uncle Jim was never around to admire his handiwork.

I kept the clippings. They might make for good horror comics some day. And if you're waiting for me to say the other reason Uncle Jim might have called was because the Gravedigger had his paws on something bigger than a little seed of truth about Johnny—you'll be waiting a long time.

43

Chapter Five

Marcy wrote to me from Pugwash. It wasn't a letter exactly, just a bunch of pictures she'd drawn. Marcy jumping into the pond with her cousins. Marcy's family around the campfire. That sort of thing. She'd written "a summer in Pictures" on the back of the envelope, which was covered in peppermint-pink kittens with little hearts and stars around them. Marcy's drawings were never very good, but I let her go on about how one day we'd be famous artists and live together in Gay Par-ee. Couldn't help but wonder, though, how she thought she was going to get from pink kittens to Picasso.

I sat on the porch with my favourite number 3 pencil and Stillman's number 2 pad, trying to draw a letter back. Somehow I didn't feel like doing Mama tumbling down the stairs. And I figured the most truthful way to tell Marcy about the

Gravedigger was to just leave him out of the picture. If I had my way, he'd be gone before she got back. Instead, I decided to draw the Ragman.

The Ragman was leading his old horse up the street. He called, "Rags, get out yer rags!" The cart was heaped with clothes, and the horse's flanks were glistening with sweat. "Rags, get out yer rags!"

The Ragman was just about the only black person you saw on Agricola in the summertime, except for maybe the kindergarten teacher, Miss June, who lived over on Creighton Street. She always spent a whole week decorating the classroom before the first day of school. During the school year, a lot of the black kids had to be bused in from Africville on an Acadian Lines bus. Didn't seem fair, when the rest of us just meandered up the street. The Ragman came from Africville, too. He looked exactly like a white kid in my class named Ben Buchanan. Have you ever seen that? Two people who look alike except for something real obvious on the surface? You point that sort of thing out to people and they say, "No, he don't. Ragman's black. He's got black hair and brown skin and brown eyes. Ben Buchanan's got blond hair and white skin and blue eyes." But both of them had long eyelashes, and their cheeks pulled taut when they smiled and made three deep lines. And they both had big front teeth, but big in a nice way, and pointy chins. And when everything

45

started working together—eyes, cheeks, lines, teeth—their faces made the same triangle. But if you point that out to people they say, "No, he don't. Ragman's black." It's enough to turn your kittens pink.

The screen door creaked open. Mama leaned over Norman's umbrella and held out her coin purse. "Go to the store and get two pounds of ground steak," she said. "Tell Jack Newberry that if he sends you home with something fatty, it will be trotted right back to him."

Lord, I'd been to the butcher's just that morning. And the day before. And every day since I was old enough to walk to the end of the block by myself. Another mother might say to herself, "Gee, I wonder if I ought to get a little ground steak since my kid is already fetching bacon." Not my mother. Jack Newberry liked to tell the other customers that I had a little crush on him and that's why I went so often. I hated that.

"It's too hot, Mama. Do I have to go now?"

"Yes."

"Do I have to go right now?"

"Yes."

"Why?"

"Because I said so."

That was the law in our house, Mama saying so. Always and forever. Martha was five when I was born and Young Lil was ten. Doris was fourteen, Margaret was seventeen, and Freddie was twenty. They're old now, the whole lot of them, but they still do what Mama says-so.

"Back again?" said Jack Newberry. "Why aren't you off playing with the other kids?"

I shrugged. Jack Newberry put the ground steak on the scale. The stiff cold coming from the freezer felt good on my skin. I'd have pressed my whole self against the nice cool display case, except for the cows' tongues and pigs' hoofs on the other side of the glass.

There were other customers lining up, but he let me look at the ground steak before he wrapped it. Then I gave him the money and braced myself for the heat outside. Just as I was pushing on the door, Jack Newberry said—

"Rosalie?"

"Yes, sir?"

"You're here so often I'm beginning to think you've got a little crush on me."

I could hear them all chuckling as the door shut behind me.

Pauline Christianson and Katie Price were sitting outside of Millner's, sucking on Popsicles, a pile of empty wrappers and sticks between them on the bench. They were Marcy's and my best school friends. In the winter, we'd go down to Pauline's basement, where her father hung salt cod to dry from the ceiling, and have ourselves a little salt-cod snack with a bit of toothpaste smeared on each bite.

"Rosalie! You going down to the lake later?" Pauline called.

"Nope."

"Just come sit by the water," said Katie. "Here, want half of my Popsicle? I got an orange one by mistake."

I didn't like orange either, but I wasn't going to turn down a free Popsicle.

"I suppose you heard I can't go too far from home these days," I said.

"Oh, your mother!" said Pauline. "Did she really break her leg? In two?"

"Yeah, sort of. Got a cast and everything. She fell down the stairs. I heard her go, too."

"Oh no!"

"Yup."

"Did you hear her bone snap?" You could tell by the way Katie glanced down at the pile of Popsicle sticks that she was this close to using one to make her point. But she thought better of it.

"Well, I heard something like a snap, but I don't know what it was exactly."

"God!"

"Ew!"

"It was right scary," I said. "But I looked over her until we could get her to the hospital."

"You're like a hero," said Pauline.

"Well . . ."

"You are!"

"You'd have done the same. You know, your heart starts pumping what with the fright of it, but your body knows what to do, so you just do what you have to do, and . . ."

Ever stop listening to yourself right in the middle of talking? My mouth was going on about how people been known to lift cars off someone because their fear gives them superhuman strength, and maybe that's where the inspiration for Superman came from, because didn't he do that in the first comic, when he was just a little kid, not that I was comparing myself to Superman. Meanwhile, another part of my brain had got itself up and wandered off a ways. What it was thinking about was the Gravedigger. It was thinking: Hold on a sec. What about that letter? The one that came from Ship Harbour and went to the Flynns' house by mistake. It was probably full of ordinary news from Aunt Izzie, and maybe there was something in it about Johnny. Something that might make the Gravedigger think he could get me going. Something that might make him think his lie would work out differently than it did. What if I could trick him into admitting he'd read the letter—steamed it open, maybe, like in my new favourite comic, *Detective Fantastic*? If I could prove the Gravedigger had got into our mail, I bet I could convince my parents to send him away.

After I got my superhero self home and brushed the orange off my teeth, I grabbed my shoebox full of markers and pencils. Martha was at the kitchen counter, coating a cake pan with lard. Mama was darning one of Norman's socks. I still wasn't used to seeing Mama sitting so much. The bruise on her face was fading into a mishmash of browns.

"For the love of Pete," Mama said, pulling a rolled bill out of the sock toe.

Norman was forever hiding money. He wasn't supposed to—Mama was always afraid of being robbed—but he said he felt better when he could put his hands on it. "Safe place, my eye," Mama said. "Course he'd keep a ten in the one with the hole in it."

She sighed, tucking the bill into her apron pocket.

"I was thinking that maybe I'd draw something on your cast," I said to Mama. "If you like."

"It's hard enough to keep it clean," said Mama.

"Oh, a little decoration is better looking than just plain old white," said Martha. "What would you put there? Maybe some flowers, Mama?"

Mama shrugged. "I suppose you could do a small rose or something. Just on the inside there, not on the front."

I started sketching out the rose on Mama's cast. The plaster was hard and bumpy. I had to use the eraser a couple of times and tried not to press too hard on Mama's leg.

"So how's Izzie doing these days?" I said, blowing some eraser dust off the cast.

"*Aunt* Izzie. Don't be cheeky."

"How's *Aunt* Izzie doing?"

"She's got a lot of worries."

"Things okay at the gas station?"

"Hmph. Money's tight, as usual."

"Why don't the Kellocks come for Sunday dinner any more?"

"Aunt Izzie needs Sunday just to catch up with the housework. Now there's something my father never liked us to do—work on Sundays. Used to get on Norman about it. Truth be told, he could get a little rough, your granddad, especially after Mother died and he took to the bottle. But he had a healthy respect for God, all right."

"Well, anyway," I said, "seeing's how you're laid up, maybe the Kellocks will find a way to come for a visit. Hey, you hear from Aunt Izzie lately?"

"Your father was just out there. Careful, you're colouring outside the line."

"Oh, sorry." I fixed the rose's stem with a sharp black marker. "I guess I mean a letter. I thought maybe I saw a letter from Ship Harbour last week."

Mama stuck out her foot and admired the finished rose. Then she pulled herself up with Norman's big black umbrella, which she kept hooked on the back of her chair. "No," she said, tapping out of the kitchen. "It's been a while since we had a letter."

Chapter Six

The Gravedigger was turning over the compost heap in the far corner of the yard. He stood inside the chicken wire, spearing the soggy top layer and moving it off to one side, then wedging the pitchfork underneath the good fertilizer at the bottom. Norman could do all this with a flick of his wrist, but then he was taller than the Gravedigger and had been doing it since he was born.

"What are you doing?" I asked.

It might have come out of me a little critical-sounding. The Gravedigger didn't say anything. I picked up a stray eggshell and tossed it towards the back of the compost heap where the new stuff was piled up.

"You go to the R.C. school," I said.

Nothing. Just the sucking sound of the pitchfork being pulled out the earth and then the thwack of it going back in.

"You not talking?"

"You gonna ask me a for-real question?"

"I was just wondering if you're a Mi—of the Catholic faith."

"Don't go to church."

"Didn't you go to St. Stephen's?"

"Sometimes."

The pitchfork went *shoook. Thwack. Shoook. Thwack.*

"You'd rather be working, eh?"

"I guess."

"Your brothers both working?"

"Yeah."

"Down at the shipyard?"

The Gravedigger leaned on his pitchfork. "You mean like your *cousin?*" I waited some time on the "I told you so," but it never came. "How old is he?"

"Johnny? I think he's seventeen now."

"Old enough. I suppose this means you decided I wasn't making that up."

Well, I hadn't decided anything. But I'd been thinking about it—*hard*—for a whole day. The one thing I knew for certain was that I'd held a letter in my hands. It was thick and I could picture the careful, loopy handwriting and the return address that said Ship Harbour. And I remembered about how grown-ups like to put a coat of sugar on things, especially when they're

54

talking to the youngest, and how sometimes it's hard to scrape off. Because if you do scrape it off, what you might find is that Mama lied to me.

"Did you read that letter that went to your house by mistake? You know, like steam it open?"

"You think I'm Detective Fantastic or something?" the Gravedigger said. "I don't *snoop*. I just happened to be under the window when your parents were talking. Believe me, I'm real sorry about it."

"And they said Johnny was going to be away on Sunday, right? When my aunt called, she told Norman that he'd probably miss him. Right?"

Shoook. Thwack. Shoook. Thwack. For a minute, I didn't think the Gravedigger was going to answer at all. Then the pitchfork stopped, and he said, "No one's heard from him in over two weeks."

It was like I'd gulped a big gulp of water. I could feel a coldness snaking down to my stomach and pooling there. "Did they say he went off to look for work?"

The Gravedigger flicked a potato peel off the toe of his boot. "Look, it's not easy to get a job at the shipyard. I don't know if that's what your cousin's doing, but if he is, he's gonna give up soon, and then he'll come by and explain himself and help out, just like you said. If he gets a job, you'll hear about it."

"Do you—do you think your father would know him?"

"Not likely he'd take notice of some kid looking for hire."

"Maybe we could go down and ask him."

The Gravedigger looked at me severe-like. "No."

"We won't bother him, I promise. But maybe he's seen him . . ."

"I said no."

Here's the thing about my Mama. Since I was little, she's seemed as powerful as God, only more predictable. I spent my whole life up to that moment being told what was what and no explanation, thank you very much, and if that boy, that *Gravedigger*, that Mickey Mouse from across the way thought he was going to out-Mama me, he had another think coming. I had a whole lungful of air with his name on it when he said, "I'll take you down, though, if you want to have a look around."

"You'll take me?"

"We're not telling your dad, though."

"Oh, no. Of course not."

"And we'll have to find a way to get in."

It was another day before the Gravedigger would take me to the shipyard to look for my cousin. First he had to finish with the compost. Then he had to fertilize the shrubs like Norman asked. Then he had to get the tomatoes off and, no, he couldn't wait because see how they're turning already. I even helped him since it was looking like Johnny would be an old man by the time we found him.

The Gravedigger might have been right about Johnny showing up soon. And if no one was saying anything about it, maybe they weren't so worried. After all, it wasn't like Johnny to cause his parents grief for no reason. Maybe the time had come for him to break out of Ship Harbour, come to the city, and make his own way. Course, that didn't mean people wouldn't be happy if they saw me coming up our front walk with him, and probably they'd be sorry about keeping secrets. And something else. I'd sent Mama flying down those stairs and this was a way of making things right again. Maybe. I didn't want to miss my chance.

Later that afternoon, the Gravedigger came back to the house and said, "All right. We're going."

Mama and Martha were having tea in the kitchen. I told them about how David had never been swimming and wasn't that a shame, and shouldn't I take him out to Chocolate Lake, meet up with some of the other kids, get a little sunshine. And all.

Mama looked at me and then she looked at the Gravedigger. "You both finished your chores?"

"Yeah, sure."

"Rosalie did a good job with the dusting," said Martha.

"And now you want to go swimming? Rosalie, you hate swimming."

I saw Martha nudge Mama with her elbow. "Nice day to be outdoors," she said. "You'd have to be careful with your glasses, Rosalie. David, do you have something to wear in the water?" The Gravedigger nodded, scowling. "You want me to wash your overshirt while you're gone? It'll be dry by the time you get back." Martha paused. "That is, assuming it's okay with Mama."

"All right, then," said Mama. She didn't look convinced about my sudden love of the water, but there was no good reason to say no. Course, Mama always found a way to say no.

"Rosalie, no—"

"Eating before we go swimming."

"And no—"

"Frigging around with those big kids from the high school."

"And no—"

"Swimming off by ourselves because that's how people get drownded."

"Drowned. Go on, then, smarty-pants."

I pulled the Gravedigger out of the kitchen before she could change her mind. "Wait here," I said at the front stairs and ran up to my room to change into my bathing suit. I shoved towels and comic books and other lake things into two bags and ran back down again.

"You can take Archie and I'll take Bugs Bunny and then we'll switch," I said loudly enough for Mama and Martha to hear. "I got some allowance for a pop afterwards, but no drinking before we go in, just like Mama says. Now, uh, David, pass me that shirt."

I held out my hand. David peeled off his overshirt and gave it to me, then he grabbed one of the bags and headed outside.

"Bye, lovey," said Martha, as I ran back to the kitchen with the smelly laundry.

"Behave," said Mama.

"We will!"

I whooped as we turned the corner onto Kane Street. I was high from our big escape, but David was quiet.

"We'll be quick," I said. "And we won't bother your father, promise."

He stopped walking. "Let's get one thing straight. You can lie to your mum all you want, miss. You can tell people I spread kittens on my toast for breakfast, and you can pass me by on the street like you don't even see me. But don't you *ever* go telling people I can't *swim*, or you'll catch it. Get it?"

"I didn't mean—"

"I was the best swimmer at St. Stephen's, any of those choir-boys will tell you. I can do a perfect jackknife dive."

"Really? A jackknife?"

"I'll show you some time. If we ever go to the lake for real."

"Okay."

And just like that, we were walking again. For a second, I was sorry we weren't heading to Chocolate Lake after all.

The humidity had lifted, and the sun felt good on my shoulders, and the bathing suit under my clothes gave me that fun's-a-coming feeling even though we weren't really heading to a lake. A yellow tram growled past us on Gottingen Street. If I was with Marcy, we'd go down a little farther so I could have a look in the shop windows. We chose most of our clothes out of the Eaton's catalogue, so the only shopping ever I did was when Mama sent me to the store's order department with a list.

The problem was, David said, as we skidded down to Barrington Street, the shipyard had a fence and a guardhouse and a guard. You didn't get in without an ID card. Sure, there were lots of people who would've liked to have a look around, maybe pick up some tools or equipment or something to trade with their buddies. Every now and then the guard might check a worker's truck on the way out to make sure he wasn't sneaking out a "rabbit"—something you made on the boss's time and the boss's nickel but kept for your own self.

There's a concrete wall that runs along Barrington Street to keep you from falling to your death on the railroad tracks below. We passed through a gap in the wall and took a latticework bridge over the tracks. A long set of stairs—must have been a hundred steps—went down, down to the entrance to the yard.

"So how do you think Johnny'd get in?" I asked.

"He'd have to fix it with someone ahead of time. You think maybe he's got a friend who works there?"

"I dunno. Johnny's lived in Ship Harbour since he was twelve," I said. "Course, everyone loves Johnny. He could be sitting beside someone on a tram one day and there you go—" I snapped my fingers. "That person'd offer him a job."

"You don't say," said David.

"Sure."

"Then I figure alls we have to do is get inside and look for the big Johnny Parade."

At the entrance, a knot of workers was making their way past the guardhouse, showing their ID cards. We waited until they were through, then David marched right up to the guard.

"Allo, David!"

"Hey, François."

The guard, François, was a big guy with a big blond moustache and a plaid cap pushed back on his head. "You come in to work, eh?" He laughed. I didn't think it was all that funny, but David laughed, too.

"No, sir, I'm just looking for my dad."

"You want me to get him? I can't go until the other guy comes back."

"Ah, shoot. You can't let us through just for a sec? I gotta be somewhere." David nodded in my direction.

"Can't keep the lady waiting, eh?" François laughed again. I fidgeted with my bag. "Sorry, but no way. I tell him you come by?"

"Nah, that's all right," said David. "It was supposed to be a surprise, you know."

François looked stricken. "I tell you what," he said. "I'm just doing my job, right? I don't make the rules. Okay, sometimes I'm busy and I don't notice something. So what?" He gestured in a *tres François* kind of way. "I do my best, you know? I do my job."

"Gotcha," said David. "Thanks anyway, François." He said it kind of loudly. "We'll get out of your way." A truck was pulling up to the entrance.

"Okay, you kids have good times."

I was peeved, to say the least. "This is how you sneak into places? You ask the gatekeeper straight out and then talk loud enough for half the shipyard to know that we're trying to get in?"

"Keep your voice down."

"Keep my voice down!"

David grabbed my arm and pulled me around the truck. "Lord jumpin', girl," he hissed. "Shut yer yap for a second."

He lifted a tarp draped over the truck bed. "Empty," he said. A quick look around, and next thing you knew, he'd scrambled up and disappeared into the back.

"Hurry up," said the tarp.

"Are you crazy?"

David poked his head out. "She's gonna move in three seconds and there's two more trucks coming this way. You want to find your cousin?"

The truck grumbled into gear.

I put my foot on the bumper and grabbed the Gravedigger's outstretched hand.

Chapter Seven

The truck did a lot of lurching and swerving and smelling like gasoline and dog fur. It was hot under the tarp. My knees burned on the metal truck bed. My hand rested on something greasy. I could feel David breathing. I wondered if he was scared, but when we bumped around a corner he put his hand on my back and kept me steady.

We stopped. The truck rocked as the driver's door opened and slammed shut. After a minute, David stuck his head out and looked around. Then he flung back the tarp, and we climbed out and dusted ourselves off.

There's this old comic—the only time I ever saw Halifax in one—about Johnny Canuck battling infamous war criminal Rudolf Hindor, who was using brain serum and radio magnetic rays to control the minds of his private army and threaten the world. I mean, *Threaten the World!!!* Hindor's army was stealing planes and ships from along the coast, and let me tell you, when you're standing there in the shipyard you realize just how hard a time they must have had of it.

Rising above us was a gigantic ship that filled the whole sky with steel. I just about fell over trying to see all the way to the top. The ship was sitting in an enormous hole in the ground—the dry dock, David called it. Way down in the hole, workers were leaning out from wood scaffolding, tickling the ship's belly with paintbrushes. The air smelled like paint fumes and hot metal and salt, and a strong breeze off the water snatched at my breath.

"Better start with the main building," said David. We made our way towards it, ducking behind oil drums and a pile of large steel beams. People noticed all right, but no one stopped us. David watched for his father. And I watched for Johnny.

"Tell me again what your cousin looks like," said David.

Across the yard, a huge crane was lowering a boiler into the keel of a new ship. The ship was built only to about where the first deck would begin. It looked like the world's biggest gravy boat.

"I'd say Johnny's about seven feet tall," I said. "He has night-black hair and sky-blue eyes."

"Are you kidding me? Seven feet tall? You think maybe he just seemed that way 'cause you were shorter the last time you saw him?"

I thought back. "Maybe he's six-foot-something."

David said something under his breath. Might have been "Lord love us," but then a sick look came over his face.

"What the heck are you doing here?"

Soon as I turned around, I knew it was one of David's brothers. Gerry, maybe. He had the same black curls and the same mean look in his eye. His chin jutted out when he was mad, just like David's did now. They were like two sides of a mirror, only a bendy mirror that made the Gravedigger look a lot smaller.

David said, "We're trying to find somebody."

"How'd you get in?"

"Walked in." His brother crossed his arms. David held his stare for a second then looked away. "Snuck in."

"You'd better sneak back out again before Dad sees you."

"We got business here."

"Oh, yeah? What kind of business?"

David didn't say anything. His brother looked at me. "This one of the Norman girls? Key-rist, Dad is going to kill you, and then her dad is going to kill you all over again. You get her out of here. This isn't no place for a girl."

David toed the ground for a second. He tapped my elbow. "Let's go."

Something I knew about David by now was that he had three walks. A stomp, a shuffle, and when he was pleased with himself,

66

like a bear up on its hind legs—sort of light on his heels, and I can't describe it any better than that. When he suddenly turned and walked back to where we'd left his brother, it was a five-alarm stomp. I couldn't hear what David said to him, but when he finished he crossed his arms and looked like he'd grown an inch.

His brother called me over. "All right. What's he look like, this cousin of yours?"

David nudged me.

"He's about six-foot-something and has night-black hair and, um, regular blue eyes," I said. "His name's Johnny Kellock. Have you seen anyone who fits that description?"

"I almost fit that description."

"He's not near as strong-looking as you."

"No, don't imagine. Okay, fine. I'll keep an eye out. Now, you two better go. I'll take you out."

David started to say something, but his brother cut him off. "You weren't here," he said.

David's brother—who was Gerry—drove us out in a van. Thankfully, no one stopped him at the guardhouse to check for rabbits. After climbing the long set of stairs back up to street level, then the steep hill you had to face no matter where you turned off Barrington, my legs were burning like crazy. If David hurt as bad as I did, he didn't say. It was clear enough he was mad at me for getting him in trouble. Maybe Gerry would keep an eye out for Johnny. But maybe the Gravedigger's helping days were through.

I was so absorbed in my thoughts, I didn't notice David step off the sidewalk, and I walked headlong into a group of sailors going the other way. On summer nights, the downtown was filled with sailors in their bell-bottoms and round caps. Dark blue edged in white. The American sailors wore white uniforms with blue trim and looked like they'd stepped right out the movies. They'd come off their ships and mingle with the local girls.

Young Lil once got caught sneaking out after curfew. She was wearing her girlfriend Marianne's pink satin skirt with a crinoline and her mouth was covered with thick red lipstick. Martha and me watched the showdown from the stairs. I thought Young Lil looked like Marilyn Monroe—except for her brown hair and the way she spit a little when she yelled back at Mama—but Martha whispered that it was cheap to wear your effort on your face like that. Young Lil was grounded for a month. I wondered what punishment I'd get if Mama found out that, in just one afternoon, I'd gotten tangled up with sailors, a Frenchman, and a couple of Micks.

Before everyone was married off and busy, us Normans were always going downtown to take in a movie or just get a hamburger or an ice cream and walk around. Other times we'd take Freddie or Cecil's car out to Queensland Beach for fish and chips, or to the Chicken Burger in Bedford, where we'd take turns choosing songs on the jukebox. You always stayed out as late as you could in the summer, and even when you got home, after dark, you'd stay out on the porch a while, hoping the heat would be let out of the house by the time you went in. I don't know how it happened, but all day the house seemed cooler than the outside and then—*blam*—the outside was cooler than the house. If there's such a thing as a lousy scientific miracle, I think that's it.

When we got back to Agricola Street, David went straight home. Mama, Norman, and Martha were sitting on our front porch. Norman had his feet resting on his lunch pail.

"That was a quick swim," Martha said. "Did David have fun? He forgot to come for his clean shirt."

"I guess so."

My mind was going all over the place. I hadn't remembered to wet my hair, and would there have been time enough for it to dry, and could I run my towel under the hose without Mama noticing so I could hang it up on the line?

Norman was looking across the street. "You and David have a fight or something?"

"Oh, yeah. A big one." That part at least felt like it was true.

"You'll work it out," he said.

"Sure they will," Mama said. "If Rosalie can just learn to keep her mouth shut."

Chapter Eight

On Sunday, Martha and her friends set off for church without me. I'd told Mama I wasn't feeling well. Really, I just didn't want to face the caterwauler, but the thing about Mama is, she never bothers you about being sick. That's because Martha used to miss a lot of school on account of her asthma. One time a teacher didn't notice how she bad she was getting, and Martha almost died. Ever since then, all you had to do was say to Mama that you didn't feel good and you could stay home.

Through my bedroom window, I could hear a bunch of boys coming down the street. They were Catholic boys, dressed up in their church clothes but pushing and shoving and laughing at each other like their mothers had just let them out of their cages. It's a wonder, I thought, that girls ever got married, because you had to forgive your fiancé for once being a rotten boy.

Just as the boys were passing between our place and the Flynns', David came out of his house. He was carrying a shovel, for land's sake, holding it in front of him like he was taking a load of dirt somewhere special. Might as well have been wearing a big sign that said "Pick On Me."

"Hey, Flynn! You digging graves in your off hours?" one of the boys called.

The others laughed—put-on-like, the way you do when a joke isn't that funny and you're going to pretend it was. David just stared down at the boys like they were a bunch of maggots. But there was something about the way he was holding steady there. Too steady. I ducked my head out the window and strained to see what was going on in those green-blue eyes. He was nervous.

"I said, you're digging graves, are yah? Got yourself a fresh body in the house?" the kid called again, a little bolder this time. "Hey, Gravedigger?"

David started coming down his walk towards the boys. Real slow, real careful with that shovel. Some of them flinched back a bit, but the group held steady. Nobody was going to be the first to bolt.

"I'll be with you in a minute," David said, stepping down onto the sidewalk. "Only first I've got these little graves to dig. Small ones. Teeny. Tiny."

He suddenly thrust the shovel towards the boys, and—oh my—didn't that send them screaming and running, because just for a second there, it looked like the Gravedigger might lose the load of dead mice that was balanced on the end of it.

From somewhere inside the house, Norman chuckled.

A mouse had fallen onto the sidewalk, and David had to bend low to scoop up its little grey body without dropping the others. He didn't even glance in my direction, just shuffled back up his walk and took his corpses around the back. I hoped the part about burying them was true.

I found Norman downstairs, rinsing out wash rags at the kitchen sink. He was wearing one of Mama's aprons.

"If your mother finds streaks on those front windows, you're going to cover for me, right?"

"Yup."

"The Flynn boy's been doing such a good job, I don't know what else I'm going to do with myself today. Might have to pray or something." He suddenly started at the sight of something out in the garden, his whole self going stiff like a hunting dog. "*Cats*," he said, dropping his hands back into the water.

I held up my sketch pad so he could see the portrait of Margaret's wedding that I'd copied from the photograph. As it turned out, Johnny was the tallest person in the picture besides the groom. Course, that wasn't saying a lot, in our family.

"Don't know where you got the knack," Norman said. "Weren't from me. Remember when you lost the locket Margaret gave you for being a flower girl?"

I rolled my eyes. I'd taken an earful about that one. No one ever let me forget anything.

"Aw. People are so hard on the baby." He patted my head with a wet hand. "Speaking of the Flynn boy, Bean, what's that the kids call him again?"

"Um . . . the Gravedigger."

"Why is that?"

"'Cause he works over at the cemetery. You know, where his mum's buried." I didn't tell Norman about how people said the Gravedigger had dug his mother up. It seemed pretty silly, anyway, now that I kind of knew David.

"Don't imagine anyone's quite right who loses their mother that way."

"What way?"

Norman wiped his hands on Mama's apron. Then he took it off and hung it to dry by the warming hub of the stove. "Too young. She drowned, you know."

If you're going to die before your time, I don't suppose drowning's worse than sickness or a train wreck or falling off a cliff. But it's still shocking somehow, especially when it happens to someone who knew someone you know. Maybe it's because when people drown, you figure most of them know it's happening. They can *feel* themselves dying. If you fall off a cliff, well, let's hope you hit bottom before your brain catches up with the rest of you.

"How did it happen?" I asked.

"I don't think you need to hear another story about people drowning. Anyway, who's that sneaking into the house?"

Storming in was more like it. Freddie, his wife, Hazel, Margaret, and her husband, Cecil, had let themselves in the front, and the kitchen door swung open with a bang.

"Number one and two," Norman said brightly. "Aren't you a sight for sore eyes."

Martha, home from church, brought up the rear.

"We'd have got here sooner," Freddie said, "but we thought we'd try an extra, *extra* slow route today."

Margaret's icebox eyes made it clear what the fight had been about.

"Well, sir," said Norman, "lovely day for a drive."

"Hello, lovey," Cecil whispered. He bent down and gave me a quick kiss on each cheek. Cecil went to Europe once. "One from your niece and one from your nephew. They're at their other grandmother's today."

"Maybe if *your wife* had let us roll down the windows for two minutes, the car wouldn't have filled up with *smoke,* and we could've *seen* where we were *going*," Margaret said, her voice rising higher with each word.

Hazel, every hair in place, sniffed a thin, rasping sniff. She shot Margaret a poisonous look before blowing a stream of smoke in her direction.

"Maybe you oughta take your own car next time!" Freddie boomed. "Wouldn't you say, Norman?"

Norman was frowning at his watch and tapping it as if it was broken, although I could see plain as anything the second hand was moving around.

"Good Lord. Can't you fight in your own homes!" They all gasped at the sight of Mama, with her cast, standing in the doorway, leaning on Norman's umbrella. "I'm fine," she said, waving away the hands trying to help her to a chair. She propped up her cast on the sewing box.

"Remind me," said Freddie, "how the heck you did this."

I slipped beside Norman in the corner rocking chair and tried to make myself invisible.

"Tripped on the stairs," Mama said, smoothing down the front of her housedress.

"And . . ." Margaret prompted.

Mama shrugged. "I landed."

Her face was set. She wasn't going to say any more.

Freddie looked at Margaret, who raised an eyebrow. "Mama, you should be more careful."

"Thank you, son. I'll keep that in mind."

Cecil turned his head away. I think he was smiling. I might have, too, but I was caught up in how Mama hadn't told them about the pencils. She wasn't going to say the accident was my fault. Maybe it really was knocked out of her memory. And everyone believed her. Even Hazel just shook her head and took another drag on her cigarette.

"You weren't expecting a Sunday dinner, were you?" said Mama. "We're not cooking for crowds these days."

"No, Mama," said Margaret. "Just wanted to see how you were getting along."

"Fine."

"Are you in pain?"

"No."

"No?"

"Well, the cast is damn itchy."

Margaret and Freddie looked at each other again. They both seemed to be waiting for the other to say something.

"For the love of God, someone spit it out," said Mama.

"You remember that lot we stopped by, out Prospect way?" Cecil said to Norman. "When my pal Dale was looking to buy outside the city?"

"Sure, sure," said Norman.

"It's back on the market. There's a nice little house on it now and I hear there's Crown land behind."

"That's a beautiful lot," said Norman.

"Made us think of you, that's all."

"Where are you kids going with this?" said Mama.

"Nowhere," said Freddie. "Some people just think that you might do better in a house with one floor."

"Some people do, do they?"

"Why not make it easier on yourself? Once Martha goes off and gets married, there will only be three of you. You can't be depending on Rosalie."

The mountain of words that piled up in my brain was so huge I couldn't even get a foothold. I felt Norman's arm tighten around me.

"We'll manage, thank you," said Mama. "You forget the aunties stayed here until they died."

After my grandmother passed on, people said my granddad couldn't raise his kids on his own. That's how Mama, Aunt Izzie, and Uncle Jim ended up here. If Mama died, I couldn't imagine leaving Norman to go to live with someone else, especially two old gnarled-up great-aunties who made you earn your keep by doing chores from morning till night. Mama took care of the aunties until the end, when they caught the same flu and died

78

within a few days of each other. We're not supposed to say a word against them, mind, since they left Mama the house.

"The aunties had you helping them, didn't they?" said Freddie. "These girls aren't going to stay in this house any more than Johnny's going to stay in Ship Harbour his whole life to help run that station. You and Izzie got to start thinking ahead."

"I think you'll be waiting a long time to see me married," Martha said quietly.

"Why? You're good-looking enough."

Martha's mouth opened, but no words came out. Couldn't get a foothold, I guess. Or maybe the smoke was getting to her, because she just smiled, plucked her white church gloves off the counter, and glided out of the kitchen.

"Speaking of Johnny . . ." Norman began. I twisted around in the chair so I could see his face. "Oh. Well. Rosalie drew a real nice picture of him."

"Goody for Baby," said Hazel.

"Bean."

I dog-eared the copy of *Richie Rich* I was reading and put it on my bedside table. "We're not going to move, are we?"

"Aw. That's just talk."

"Okay."

"Always wanted a big yard for you kids. And a better garden for Mama. But I probably don't got enough squared away for a lot as nice as that one."

"That's good. I mean, I don't want to move."

"Yeah, moving's hard when you're young."

We sat quietly for a bit. When you grow up with about a hundred kids in your family, probably the best thing you could wish for would be a nice place of your own to live in, and here I'd just said no to it, like I had any say-so.

I didn't know how not to talk to Norman about something. Not telling him what I knew about Johnny was like having an itch you can't scratch under a cast. But I wanted him to tell me. And something else. If something's so big it's too big to talk about over cigarettes at Mama's kitchen table, well, maybe I didn't want to know the whole truth of it yet.

"Funny when Hazel dropped that spoon in her teacup, wasn't it?" said Norman.

"Yeah," I said. "Tea flew up her nose."

Norman creaked his old self down the hall, and I lay in bed not-sleeping. After a long while, I turned on my flashlight and tried thinking up a new comic strip, but it just wouldn't come.

Chapter Nine

Martha and I set out for the Hydrostone Market first thing. Martha wanted to get the week's shopping over with before she had to go to work. We had a long, mixed-up list— thread, Noxema, shoe polish, butter. I wondered if David would be at the house when we got back.

"Rosalie!" Mama called from the chesterfield, just before the screen door closed behind us. "On your way back, pick up two pounds of ground steak. Tell Jack Newberry if he sends you home with something fatty, it will be trotted right back to him."

"Yes, Mama!" Martha called back. She pushed me down the porch steps before I could be smart.

On the way to the Hydrostone, I told Martha about my conversation with Norman the night before. "We probably don't have enough money to buy that place Cecil was going on about," I said. "So I guess that's that."

"I wouldn't be so sure."

"What do you mean?"

"We'd sell our house, of course. And you know that big cigar box where Norman keeps the extra bullets for his hunting gun?"

"Yup." We weren't supposed to touch that box.

"*Yes*," Martha corrected me. "He's been putting money in there for years."

"How do you know?"

"I dropped it once when I was cleaning. I'd wager even Mama doesn't know how much is in there."

"How much?"

"I don't know, either. But that was a long time ago and there was a lot even then."

"Are you saying we got enough to buy that lot?" I could feel my chest getting tight just thinking about leaving our house. I know houses don't have feelings, but it seemed cruel to just up and go as soon as we could afford something better. I knew every inch of that old place. We'd all been born there. And the aunties had died there. And, anyway, where would I go to school? What would I do without Marcy? How could we ever leave the North End? Aw geez, going to the butcher wasn't so bad.

"If Norman says we're not moving, we're not moving," Martha said. "It's just that money may not be the issue."

"Do *you* want to move?"

"I'm going to university in a year, remember? That's a promise I'm going to keep no matter where the family lives."

Promised our parents, I guess. Martha was going to be the first of us Normans to get a university degree—and maybe the last. I was kind of hoping I'd make it big as an artist without going through all that.

Hardly anyone was at the Hydrostone yet, and we ticked off our list lickety-split. While Martha was in Mr. Butt's drugstore buying Noxema for Mama, I drifted across the street to the Blue Nose Diner. The menu was posted high in the window and I stretched up on my toes to read the beverage section. I thought maybe Martha could be convinced to buy me a milkshake before we headed home. We could sit at the counter, just like the kids in the *Bobbysoxers* comics, swirling the foamy chocolate around in cold, heavy glasses.

On the other side of the window, someone was sitting at a table, hunched over a newspaper. Even from that angle I knew it was David. There were empty plates and cups on the table, like he'd been eating with other people and he was the last to leave. But who would be hanging out with the Gravedigger? And what kid—other than us—would be down at the Hydrostone this early in the summertime?

"Rosalie, please don't stare at those poor people trying to have their breakfast."

"David's been hanging out here with someone," I told Martha. "I didn't think he had any friends."

"Aren't you his friend?"

I gave her my best Mama-look.

"Maybe he had breakfast with his family, then. Didn't one of his brothers work here before he got on at the shipyard?"

"How'd you know that? You know his brothers?" My chest tightened.

"Just enough to give a wave," said Martha. "One of the other girls at the library used to go out with his brother Tom in high school. She thought he was quite a catch."

Before they moved to Agricola, the Flynns used to live near the big Sears store. I thought back to what Norman said about moving being hard when you're young. Maybe the Gravedigger wasn't even the Gravedigger at his old school, St. Agnes. Maybe he was just David. The only times I ever saw him with other people was when he headed out in the morning with his father and brothers.

"Never would have thought the Flynns eat their breakfast at a restaurant," I said.

"A houseful of bachelors?" Martha laughed. "This may be their one square meal of the day. You want to go in for a cold drink?"

"Not if David's not speaking to me."

"You two . . . Good thing I got us a couple of pops, then. We could have them up at Fort Needham, if we don't dawdle . . . Here, help me sort out these bags so they're easier to carry."

Fort Needham is this hill near the Hydrostone. It's not as big as Citadel Hill, which overlooks the whole city. And Citadel Hill has a fort on it, while Fort Needham only has grass and berries and cigarette butts. Just about every boy in the North End learned to smoke up on Fort Needham. But it's a pretty steep hill, all the same, and you can see the harbour from the top.

"Johnny and I used to come up here a lot, back when the Kellocks lived in the city," Martha said as we turned onto the path. "Do you remember us taking you sledding here?"

"Sure. I laughed so hard once, I peed my pants."

"Oh, yes! Johnny told Mama it was his fault. He said he picked you up and squeezed you too hard in the middle."

"I don't remember that part."

"You were little."

Martha's asthma was acting up. I took a shopping bag from her.

"I'll tell you one of my earliest memories," she said. "It was the first day of school. And I was sick again—must have missed half of kindergarten. I was at home, on the landing. Clutching my doll." She paused for breath. "The doctor came downstairs and he told me. About the real live baby I could take care of. From then on. I asked him where it came from. And he pointed. To his black bag."

I laughed. Martha laughed, too. "After that," she said, "I didn't mind being home. Because I always had company." She stepped aside to let a man go by us on the path.

"You've got company now," the man said. He was old, maybe thirty. His face was clean-shaven, but he had a smell like he hadn't had a bath for a while. Reminded me of Rock Hudson, only leaner and rough-looking.

"Why don't you hand over your purse, lady," he said to Martha. "I've got a knife."

He twitched his hand inside his jacket pocket. Martha didn't move. She just stood there wheezing. I looked around, frantically. The man was blocking the path below us. There was no one else around. And from below it would have just looked like three people talking.

"Come on, let's have it," the man said.

Martha passed the rest of the shopping bags to me with shaky hands and slipped her purse off her shoulder. Then, before I realized what was happening, the purse was swinging and it clunked the man upside of his skull. He staggered backward and fell, a surprised look on his face, and Martha pulled me by the arm up the path.

We ran and ran. Over the hill. Past the harbour and the little glimpse of the new Macdonald Bridge that you could spot between the trees if you weren't running for your life. Past the raspberry bushes and down the hill on the other side. The bags banged hard against my hipbones, but we didn't stop and we didn't look behind us until we'd made it back to the Hydrostone.

By then Martha was gasping for air so bad I thought she was going to turn blue. But she took a puff of medicine from her inhaler and after a few minutes was able to take shallow breaths. We sat on a bench with the bags dropped at our feet. "Thank God. For this brilliant invention," she panted, holding up the inhaler. And I was so relieved to see her colour coming back that all I could do was squeeze her tight.

Mama wasn't too pleased that we'd forgotten to pick up the ground steak on the way home. But Martha got her off my back by telling her what a good deal we got on the large jar of Noxema that she pulled out of her purse.

David wasn't at the house when we got back, and he never came. I was a bit sorry that I didn't have the chance to tell him what happened at Fort Needham. Aw, he probably wouldn't have believed it anyway.

That night, after Mama and Norman had gone to sleep, I slipped out of bed and crept down the hall towards Martha's room. We'd decided not to tell our parents about Rock Hudson's evil twin. We'd probably have a hard time coming and going on our own if we did. One more secret between us all. But I was tired of having Johnny between Martha and me. Maybe it was a little selfish. Johnny might come home soon, just like David said, and Martha might get upset for no reason. But maybe he wouldn't come home soon and she'd want to know that. I could tell from the way she smiled when she told that story about going sledding. There was a time, back when the Kellocks still lived in the North End, when Martha and Johnny were pretty good friends.

Martha's bed was empty. I tiptoed down the stairs towards a light coming up from the living room. I knew my sister loved this place from spending so much time at home when she was younger. It wasn't until that moment, though, that it occurred to me how she might be even more attached to our old house than I was. When I twisted my head down and peeked between the banister rungs, I saw her sitting in Norman's horsehair chair. A cigar box was open on her lap. She was holding a large bundle of money in her hands and she was crying.

Chapter Ten

I heard the Flynns' door bang shut across the road and what sounded like a rake being dragged down their stairs. I didn't look up from my sketch pad. He could come or not—didn't matter to me. It's just that a person should work on someone's yard if they say they're going to. Even if they have to hold down their creepy job at the graveyard, they should still make good on their arrangements. No one was going to make him speak to me.

David's shadow and black-pepperish smell fell over me. I tried to hold my face still, but I could feel the smile wriggling at the corners of my mouth. Then I remembered what Norman said about David's mother. My face fixed itself.

"Gerry says there's a new guy named John at the shipyard. Says he's got black hair and he's tall."

I looked up. "Did he talk to him?"

"Nah, he only seen him from across the way. But someone told him that was the guy's name."

I knew better than to ask for another favour. "That's real nice of your brother to let us know," I said. "I guess I'll look into that."

I took a pencil from the shoebox at my feet and twisted it in the little sharpener.

The rake handle pivoted slowly on the porch step.

"It's nothin' to me if we went down there again," David said.

"Where?"

"The shipyard."

"Oh, yeah?"

"Gerry says if we meet him there late this afternoon, he'll get us in. If you want. All the same to me."

We made a plan.

I asked Mama if we could go down to Nelson Seed to see Norman. David gave me the excuse that we were running low on fertilizer for the garden and we needed to pick some up. According to the plan, we would buy extra time at the shipyard by saying we stopped for a pop somewhere on the way home. Course, that didn't get me far.

"You can tell Norman what you need tonight," Mama said, "and he'll bring it home tomorrow. I don't want you bothering him at work."

My first instinct was to keep at her, but I shut my yap. I'd been watching how Martha got around Mama. She always came in the side door, if you know what I mean. Like how she helped us to go swimming at Chocolate Lake by telling Mama what a good job we'd done with our chores. I felt a little guilty about that. In a way, I'd made Martha lie.

So I didn't fuss when Mama said we couldn't go. I let her get settled on the chesterfield with her tea and her sewing and got right to my chores.

They who tread the path of labor follow where my feet have trod;
they who work without complaining, do the holy will of God . . .

"What's that noise?" Mama called.

"I been thinking about joining the junior church choir," I said. "I got to practise!"

I worked my way through an afternoon's worth of hymns. I sang "When the Day of Toil is Done" while I did the dishes and "Thy Glorious Work, O Christ, is Done" while I did the floors. Before I finished the dusting, I'd run through "Welcome, Sweet Day of Rest," "For all the Saints Who From Their Labors Rest," and "When we our Wearied Limbs to Rest."

"I'm off to collect my paycheque!" Martha yelled over "O Where Shall Rest Be Found."

"They don't usually have them ready till the end of the day," said Mama.

"I just remembered, Mrs. Johnson wants me to drop by a little early."

"You be careful," Mama said. "Rosalie, hush for a second. This goes for you, too. They told on the radio this morning that a man was assaulted at Fort Needham yesterday in broad daylight. Broad daylight, girls . . . Girls! What's so funny?"

After "Lord, Dismiss Us With Thy Blessing," Mama called me into the living room.

"Seems Martha forgot to put a piece of apple cake in Norman's lunch. You know he won't last until supper without a snack. Better take it down to him."

"But, Mama, who's going to stay with you?"

"Tell Mag Hewitt on your way out that she can stop in for tea, after all. And Rosalie." Mama reached into her pocket. "Here's your allowance." She reached into her pocket again. "And maybe you ought to take David out for a hamburger and a show. He's been fussing around in that garden all day. You two shouldn't be stuck home with an old woman."

Funny, but I got a little lump in my throat when she said that.

We took a tram downtown. Trams always put me in a dreamy state of mind. One of my favourite daydreams is what the city would have been like during the war. Norman was too young to serve in the Great War and he couldn't serve in the Second World War on account of his enlarged heart. Instead, his job was to walk around during the blackouts and check that people got their blinds down and lights off. If the city was dark, the German pilots couldn't see it from the night sky. The German planes never came, but people had to be ready. I imagined Norman patrolling the streets, making sure everyone's tucked in good, that big heart thumping in his chest.

When you go into Nelson Seed, you have to stop for a second to breathe in deep. Your whole nose gets filled up with the thick, musty smell of seeds and peat. Behind the main counter are rows and rows of little wooden drawers, like tiny safety deposit boxes. After he set aside a bag of fertilizer to take home for us, Norman showed David how you could find just about anything you ever wanted to plant if you knew which drawer to slide open.

By the time we got to the shipyard, Gerry was waiting outside by his truck, looking anxious.

"Where you been?" he said. "I gotta get going."

"Aren't you going to take us in?" David said. "I had to listen to this one sing hymns half the day just to get us down here!"

"I gotta load that has to go over to Dartmouth and I'm running behind as it is. But here's the news: I talked to him."

"Who?"

"Her cousin. John."

I gasped. "You did! Where? What did he say? Is he coming home? Can I see him?"

"Whoa," said Gerry. "I don't got that much. Couldn't be too nosy without making him nervous, right? But here's what happened."

Seems Gerry ran into Johnny at the canteen on his lunch break.

"Alls I said was, 'Hey, aren't you John?' And he says, 'Sure. Pleased to meet you . . . ?' And I says, 'Gerry,' and we shake, right?

"So I says, 'I think you work with Ray Campbell, isn't that right?' And he says, 'That's right,' and I could tell from the way he was smiling and talking about the weather and stuff that he was glad to meet someone, which made me think that this guy probably just moved here, like you said."

I was shivering all over. "Did he *say* he just moved here?"

"Nah, the whistle blew and I had to go. But listen to this: we said '*See ya around.*'"

"What's the big deal about that?" said David. "Do you even know if this is the right guy?"

"I figure he is. And you know how I know?" Gerry nodded in my direction. "Because her father stopped by here this morning."

94

Norman!

"What was he doing?"

"Dunno. He was talking to Dad at the gates."

"Our dad and her dad? Was he asking about us?"

"I couldn't find out without giving away what I knew, could I?" That was a relief. At least Gerry could be trusted. "And like I said, I didn't want to make this John guy nervous. If his father's been beating the tar out of him, he's gonna be right jumpy."

All my hackles went up. "What did you say?"

Gerry looked over at David, who might have shaken his head. Just a little.

"Uh, I think . . . I got something wrong here," said Gerry. "You know some of these kids who run away, that's the reason."

"It's not like that in my family," I said. "I never saw Uncle Ezra hurt anybody."

That wasn't exactly true. One time, back when the Kellocks used to come for Sunday dinner, I saw Uncle Ezra kick Mrs. Greenwood's old dog. It wasn't doing anything, it'd just come across the street and happened to be lying at the end of our walk. As the dog ran off, howling, it struck me that Uncle Ezra didn't think of it as a living thing—it was just something in his way. I'd wanted to set him straight, but then Mama called, "Ezra, come get some stew. Try not to kick m'kid on the way in."

"Anyway," David said, "We just saw Mr. Norman. And he didn't give a sign he knew we'd been down here."

"Well, maybe he's not the person you got to watch out for right now," said Gerry. "Isn't that one of the other Norman girls coming this way?"

Chapter Eleven

Martha was carrying some books close to her chest. The wind off the harbour blew wisps of hair into her eyes. We took the chance to slip behind Gerry's truck.

She walked slowly along the road towards the entrance, but before she was even within spitting distance of the guardhouse, she turned around and headed back the other way.

"She was supposed to be picking up her paycheque at the library," I said to Gerry, who looked sort of surprised to find himself there, ducking down with us.

"She's got books, don't she?"

"Yeah, but this isn't exactly the scenic route home." I'd never known Martha to fib before, except for not telling about the Fort Needham thing.

We left Gerry to make his deliveries and trailed her, keeping back a-ways, as she slowly zigzagged her way through the North End. "I bet she's looking for Johnny," I said. "See, Norman went to the shipyard and now Martha—that proves it. Everybody knows what's going on but me."

"I don't think no one knows nothing," said David. "And this is the only place they can think of to look. If your parents haven't said anything to you, maybe it's because they think you'd make a fuss."

"I wouldn't!"

"Yeah, then what are we doing diving behind trucks?"

I thought for a second. "Because! I don't want Martha worrying we'll get her into trouble."

"Why don't you just run ahead and tell her you won't? Ask her what's going on?"

I made a face like I was considering it, taking the dare, but I couldn't really. All my life, Martha had been like a second mother to me, my nother-mother, as Norman used to joke. Only she was the kind of mother who read to me and bought me art supplies out of her small paycheque and made sure I was never left out. And now it looked as though she knew something—something important—and she hadn't told me, just like I hadn't told her. But the difference was, I knew that if I asked her about it, she'd just add another coat of sugar.

Instead, I told David about what Martha had found in Norman's cigar box. The bundle of money that was tied with a piece of string, like it was ready for the moment when someone would need it. And I found myself telling him about how Norman was hoping we could move out sometime and how I couldn't stand it, even the thought of it, leaving our old house. And how it broke my heart to see Martha crying.

"Your sister close with your cousin?" David asked.

"Martha? When they were younger, sure. But it's been a long while since he lived here."

"Oh. I was just thinking about her wandering like that."

"What about it?"

"She seems sad, is all. Or maybe lonely."

"She's probably worried about Johnny," I said. "And, besides, she has friends."

"There's something not quite right about her."

"Aw, you don't know what you're talking about."

"There was something not quite right about my mum." David took off his overshirt and busied himself tying it around his waist. "It's not the same thing, I guess."

"What do you mean . . . not quite right?"

"My brothers said she just . . . got sad one day. She never cheered up again."

"I thought—"

"What?"

"I thought she drownded. I mean, drowned."

"We were taking the ferry," David said. "All of a sudden, she let go of my hand."

Sometimes you just can't come up with the right thing to say back to a person. Sometimes the pause is so long while you think on it that you have to change the subject anyway. And sometimes, once you've done it, changed the subject, you see you've let the other person off the hook. We'd reached the Hydrostone, and we watched Martha go into the bakery. I said to David, "Let's head back. She's just doing errands and we might as well go get something to eat. If you like."

"I'm starving."

When we got to the front of the line at the Vogue Theatre, the early show was sold out. The movie was The Shaggy Dog starring Annette Funicello from the Mickey Mouse Club. Every girl with dark-brown hair wanted to be Annette Funicello. The lobby was packed with brown-haired girls. One of those girls was Nan Buckler, who technically had blond hair, but it looked darker and oilier today, like maybe she hadn't washed it so it would look more like Annette Funicello's. Nan was talking to Katie and another girl. She was probably saying tomayto tomayto tomayto. I

100

couldn't tell who the other girl was, but I could tell she wasn't Pauline, who I liked better than Katie, I decided. They didn't notice David and me before they went into the theatre. Still, I walked away from the ticket counter a little quicker than usual.

"Should we go to your house?" I asked David. "Mama's expecting it'll be getting dark by the time we get back."

I was relieved, actually, when he shook his head.

"Let's pick up some comics," he said. "Then I know somewhere we can wait it out."

You would think that, finding herself in a graveyard at dusk, a person's bones would be rattling inside her skin, but I can't say that's what happened, not even for the sake of a good story. My hair didn't turn white, my blood didn't run cold, nothing stood up on the back of my neck. I did have a nervous feeling, like when I thought of what Mama would do to me if someone were to see me here, walking over the dead like it was my own backyard. But the mist that was settling among the graves wasn't creepy at all, and the heat had relaxed the way bath water does, and the air was soft-warm.

The lights, I told myself, were just another rumour, like the ghost haunting the new Richmond School and the Gravedigger storing his mother's body in a jelly cupboard—to name two things I wished I hadn't remembered just that second.

David said, "Here she is. My mum."

The earth around the little white cross had long ago settled back into itself, and the grass around it was trimmed tidy. There was no name, no dates. Just like a weed there in the far-off corner of the graveyard. Now, I know better than to ask someone why he doesn't have his mother's name and dates on a better marker than a plain white cross. Chances are, Mama says, a person don't have something because they can't afford it, and it's not for anyone else to go pointing that out. And if maybe it's because they don't know any better, well, what makes you God's gift to education?

So I just nodded politely, like I was saying "That's real nice," which I couldn't say out loud because it would be a lie, and I should think God would get you good for telling a lie in as holy a place as a cemetery.

"I'm going to get her a big, pink stone with angels on it and a proper wreath at Christmas." David ran his hand over the cross. "Some time."

I pushed a thought out of my head then, put it aside for later, when it was a better time for thinking on those sorts of things. The thought was this: I wonder if ever, when David's mother was holding her little baby, if she ever thought about how one day, when she got old, her son would be taking care of her, and how it's a good thing, then, that we can't see into the future.

"Here, I got something to pass the time, maybe, till you can go home."

David walked over to a big tree, just down a ways from the main gates. He reached up on his toes and pulled something down from its branches.

"I made it myself." The seat was grey from the weather and the ropes were thick and dirty. "It's sturdy," said David. "I'll show you." He sat on the swing and bumped his bum on it a few times. "See, she'll hold."

At first it's scary, swinging up into the rustling blackness. But then, when you get to the top, just as high as you can go and just before you come down, the branches part, revealing a patchwork of stars. After a few swings, David slid the lantern over my arm and sent me up again, and this time the tree lit up like Christmas, and each leaf was so beautiful and so perfect, and each swing so brief and so different from the one before it that my eyes couldn't gather it all in. David pushed me again and again.

"Isn't it funny," I said on the way home, the comic books in a bag over one arm and the lantern over the other, "to think that one person feels a draft, say. Maybe a door blows open. One person thinks there's a ghost in the room, and another person thinks it's the spirit of some loved one come to check up on them. I suppose it depends on the way you look at things, but, anyway, there *are* different ways to look at things."

We were rounding the corner of Agricola Street, where the boulevard begins and splits the street in two. David took the lantern from me and extinguished the light.

"People are foolish," he said.

Chapter Twelve

Freddie got off work early on Friday to drive Mama to the doctor.

"They'll be taking this cast off today," Mama told Martha.

"I thought you had to wear it for six weeks."

"Nonsense. I told them, it's not like it was all the way broken."

Mama kept saying that as she put on her hat, sorted out her purse, went down the porch steps with Freddie. "It's not like it was all the way broken! I told them it wouldn't take so long!"

After Freddie's car pulled away, I noticed Martha went straight to the pantry and took down a box of lemon filling mix. Lemon meringue pie was Mama's favourite. The meringue part I could do without, but Mama liked the lemon, the pastry, and the meringue. It was the only thing she would sit down and eat with the rest of us until her whole piece was finished.

Martha must have thought we'd be celebrating Mama's cast coming off that night.

I'd had my eye on my sister, as Uncle Jim would say. Something had given her the idea to go to the shipyard. Had Mama and Norman told her that Johnny'd run off? Did she know Norman had been at the shipyard earlier that day? Did she know about the John who was working down there? David and I were going to find out. We had a signal. If Martha decided to go out, whoever saw first would sing (me) or whistle (David) so as to alert the other person. Then David would follow Martha and I'd tell Norman later that David had left early to take care of a "cemetery emergency."

"That's all you have to say," said David. "*Don't keep talking.*"

His eyes had followed mine to where he gripped my hand to make the point. He let go and mumbled how he had to get to the weeding. I wished there was an easy way to tell him that, actually, I was just thinking about how much cleaner his hands—his whole person, really—had been lately. Sometimes he even brought his overalls or a shirt for Martha to add to the wash. It made me wonder what would happen if Marcy came up the walk on the first day of school and this nice young feller David was sitting on the Normans' porch. Would she still see the Gravedigger?

I hung around the kitchen for a while watching Martha make the pie. She was her usual Martha-self, humming softly as she beat the egg whites, but the air felt different between us, as if we'd fought and forgiven each other but the memory of what we'd said hadn't worn off yet. And I couldn't get it out of my head how David had gone on about her seeming sad. He put it on her face like pair of glasses. Or the opposite, maybe. Like when someone who wears glasses takes them off and it's hard to keep up the conversation because you can't stop thinking about how different they look without their glasses on.

When I went upstairs for my new comics, I stood for a moment in the doorway of Martha's room. Her bed was neatly made and there were photos of her best friends, Susan and Amy, on her desk. Now that they both had boyfriends, they didn't come around like they used to. Far as I knew, Martha hadn't had a boyfriend yet. I thought about what she'd said about not getting married any time soon. What if Freddie was wrong? Maybe she would stay behind and take care of Norman and Mama, the way Mama had taken care of the aunties. Maybe she'd spend her whole life in this old house. Made me wonder all of a sudden if that was the reason Mama was always pushing us outdoors.

I could feel the summer winding down with each tick of the grandfather clock. Mama's ankle was almost better. My birthday was on Sunday, and Marcy was coming home on Monday. Then school would start. And David, he'd go off to Alexander McKay.

What if I didn't need to worry about him being at my house in September? What if he never planned to stay on?

I imagined what it might be like in a couple of weeks if me and the girls met up with David on Agricola Street. Marcy would for sure be wanting to get away, but I'd ask politely after David's brothers and his schoolwork, and I'd explain about Norman hiring David for the summer, you know, because of Mama. I'd probably smile in a knowing sort of way, a smile that says you're rolling your eyes but are too kind to do it, and the other girls' faces would melt into the same smile, and I'd try not to notice that David knew what that smile meant too.

But the thing about David is, if he ever came upon me walking with my school friends, he'd probably cross over to the other side of the street. Not because he's that rude—because he'd know what would happen, and that was almost worse.

Another thing about David: he was wrong about Johnny coming home soon. And he was the only one who could help me find him. I needed . . . a clue.

Across the hall, the faint smell of mothballs and Noxema drifted from Mama and Norman's bedroom. I tiptoed in. From the window, I could see David in the backyard below. He was pulling up weeds, cartoon-style. He pulled and pulled as though the weeds were planted in cement. As though there was some little critter burrowed under the lawn pulling on the roots and the little critter was winning. Whenever he got a weed out, he tumbled backwards, and his feet flew into the air. It was pretty clear he didn't know anyone was watching.

My hand rested near the long cedar jewellery box on Mama's dresser. Mama never wore jewellery, except for the thin, pink-gold wedding band that was her mother's. The hinges creaked a little when I opened the lid and released a cedar-y smell into the air.

It was full of letters. The printing on the envelopes was like a little kid's, some words bigger than others, sloping off the paper. It brought to mind Christmas cards and birthday wishes.

To: Mrs. Lillian Norman.
Return to: E. Kellock.

Elizabeth Kellock.
Aunt Izzie.

The envelopes had been carefully slit open and the letters re-folded and put back inside. The clock ticked. My heart thumped. I couldn't read them right there. If Martha came upstairs I might not have time to get everything back the way I found it. I tucked one into the top of my shorts and pulled my shirt down over it. I'd read it in my room with the door shut. Wait—what if Mama came home early? How would I get it back into the jewellery box? I took the letter out of my shorts. The main thing was that

I knew they were here. I'd have to find a way to get everyone out of the house so I could have a proper look.

I counted the letters. Six. All from Aunt Izzie. Underneath the letters was a jumble of little things: an old ticket stub from a movie called *The General*, a dime, a mussel shell, a dried rosebud, junk, junk, junk . . . a silver chain. I nudged the dry stem of the rosebud so I could slide the chain along the bottom of the jewellery box. On the end was a little heart-shaped locket that was bent out of shape, folded into itself.

That's when I remembered about the locket. I'd been sucking on it when Uncle Ezra was setting up the family photograph at Margaret's wedding. Johnny was telling me to hold on a minute, just wait it out, when Ezra came over and sort of pushed him back because he said I was getting mussed up. I felt my sister Doris stiffen beside me. Then Ezra's damp hands were in my hair trying to smooth it down and his funny-smelling breath was all over me, and I started to count. Afterwards, I looked down at the heart, nestled in the pink ruffles of my dress. I had almost bit it in two. So I tucked the locket beneath my collar and hid it under my pillow when I got home. When Margaret asked me later where it was, I told her I'd lost it, which seemed better somehow than saying I'd ruined it, and she got so mad.

I thought I remembered that day so clearly, but somehow I'd

forgotten that. And this, too: when I woke up in the morning, the locket wasn't under my pillow any more. I really had lost it. Except that I hadn't. Mama must have found it and kept it.

Rrrrring!

Mama's telephone went off like it knew I was back in the room. Stupid blue frog. I heard Martha running to the downstairs phone. Too close. I quickly put everything back into the jewellery box, closed the lid, and slipped out of the room. Martha's voice echoed up the stairwell: "Hello? . . . Hello?" The receiver clattered back onto its cradle.

"I thought you were going to get your comic books?" Martha asked me, as we passed each other on the stairs.

"Oh . . . I read them already."

"That's funny. I put out a little snack for you and David."

David was sitting at the kitchen table, shoving potato chips into his mouth.

"Sisters writing letters to each other," he said when I told him what I'd found. "*That's* a puzzler."

A couple of crumbs fell onto his shirt. I reached over and brushed them away and he gave me a look that would melt kryptonite.

"Excuse me, *Captain Sarcasmo*. Mama said she hadn't got any letters from Aunt Izzie in a while, and this proves she was lying."

"How old were those letters?"

"I don't know."

"Then how do we know they aren't more than a while old?"

"I don't know."

"The one that went to my house by mistake, it was there?"

I'd pushed that day as far back into my memory as I could. Now I tried to coax it out, like a stray cat. I thought of the smudge the Gravedigger's fingers had left on the envelope, the weight of the letter, the neat, loopy handwriting.

"It wasn't there!"

"You sure?"

"I'm sure of it! The handwriting's different on these ones!"

"Lord jumpin'!" David clapped a hand to his forehead. "The letter that came to my house wasn't addressed to your mother. It said Mr. and Mrs. Frederick Norman. Meaning Fred *Senior*," he added.

"I *know*. Norman Norman. I get it."

"Nah, you don't. If that letter didn't come from your aunt then it must have come from someone else in Ship Harbour, like your uncle or . . ."

We heard Martha's feet padding down the stairs.

"I'm going out for a bit," she said, as she came into the kitchen. She pulled her sunhat on. "Stay out of trouble."

Neither of us moved. The screen door bounced on its hinges. Martha's footsteps faded away.

"We been following the wrong person," David said. "Your father knows where Johnny is. I bet he's known since that letter arrived."

Chapter Thirteen

I didn't see the car pull up. I heard voices murmuring, and when I went out to the porch Mama was sitting there with Freddie and Norman. She held her purse on her lap. Her cast was propped up on Norman's lunch pail.

Norman looked like his normal self, chatting with Freddie. Not like a person with secrets. But Mama looked . . . older. Her mouth was pinched all the time these days. She'd fall heavily into a chair and grunt a little when she got up. Even the rose on her cast was faded. She'd been old for so long that I'd never thought of Mama getting older. It was like a tide rushing in, nothing you could do to push it back, it just kept coming and coming.

The oldest mother in the world. How old could she get?

"Rosa-lee, you look just like you've seen a ghost—you've seen a ghost, I say," Mrs. Hewitt called from the other side of the hedge. Her red, glistening face and fuzzy grey hair added up to something like a mouldy cranberry pudding.

"Leave her, Mag," said Mama.

"Lillian! Didn't you say that cast would be off? I'm sure you said it would be off today."

"Not today. Soon," said Norman.

"I don't mean to interrupt, of course. Just looking for Mr. Hewitt. I don't know where he's got to, I tell you, I don't know where he is."

The silence from our porch was solid as a human chain, like in a game of Red Rover. The Normans versus Mrs. Hewitt.

"Dick? Dick Hewitt, come get your supper!" she called, lumbering back to her own porch. "You don't have flesh enough to miss another!"

The telephone rang inside our house.

"Norman," Martha said, creaking open the screen door. "You need to come to the phone."

After a few minutes the door creaked again. Norman came out with Martha behind him. "I guess I'll be borrowing that car of yours, son, if you don't mind. Got to take a ride to Ship Harbour."

"You want me to go with you?" asked Freddie.

Norman nodded. "That might be a good idea."

Freddie felt for his keys in his pocket. Norman took his hat from his chair and followed my brother to the car, resting his hand for an instant on Mama's shoulder as he passed.

Martha sat down on the porch step. She rested her chin on her knees. "They're going to go get Aunt Izzie, aren't they?" she said.

Mama just sighed.

"How did you know . . . ?" I started to ask, but the question evaporated like cooking steam. Martha would have heard Norman talking on the telephone, of course, and Mama and Norman never needed many words between them.

Martha was chewing on her lip. I wished I could borrow her eyes for a while—the way you borrow a book from the library. Maybe everything would become clear. Like the time she had to explain a chapter in Little Men to me. The one where Father Baer punishes one of the boys by making him give him, Father Baer, the strap. When I looked again at the book after, it was obvious that it was a punishment the boy wouldn't soon forget, as obvious as if the author had said it straight out. Martha could always see past the surface of things. Whereas I was forever having to choose between asking a stupid question and waiting for the words to unscramble themselves.

"Mama?" I said.

She lifted her eyes to me. They were so pale the blue looked almost washed out.

"What is it?"

"Martha made a lemon meringue pie."

For just a second, the pinched look almost left Mama's face.

By the time the dishes were washed, the inside of the house was hotter than outside, so I went out onto the porch with my sketch pad. I'd been drawing so much that summer, my drawing muscle was big and bulgy on the side of my finger. But there was one picture I still wanted to do before school started. From memory. See, if I had to pick one recollection of Johnny, this would be it. I was maybe four or five—I don't remember. The rest of the family was in the living room, and they were dressed up to go somewhere. Johnny was wearing a suit jacket and a tie, and he was on the chesterfield between my sisters—I don't remember which ones—sitting in a puddle of poodle skirts. What I do remember is that easy way about him, how he sat forward with his elbows on his knees and talked like a grown-up, and how he smiled when he saw me there in my nightgown and bare feet, peeking around the doorframe.

Come to think of it, if Johnny was still living here back then, he couldn't have been older than twelve.

David shuffled over from his place and sat beside me on the step. "Saw Norman heading out. What's the matter?"

"Nothin'."

"You in a mood?"

"I don't have moods!"

He laughed. "Sure you do. Sometimes you get loud-mad and sometimes you get quiet-mad."

"Ha ha."

"At least you're not like some girls who say one thing to your face and something else behind your back."

"It's not just girls who do that."

"Girls are the worst for it, though."

Well, that was true.

"One time," David said, "in class, there was this know-it-all girl who had to recite Judge Haliburton's famous phrases from heart. And she kept looking down at her hands, like she was so shy, just the cutest. But what the teacher couldn't see was that she'd written them out on her palms. When she was finished, and she put hands behind her back, I could read one of the phrases from where I was sitting. You know what it was?" I shook my head. "*Honesty is the best policy.*"

"Ha! Ha ha! They made you learn that stuff at St. Stephen's, too?"

"Yeah."

"Us too. *You can't get blood out of stone.*"

"*Every dog has its day.*"

"*Words to live by.*"

"Nah, that's not his. His is better. It's *Live and let live.*"

We fell quiet for a second, you know how you do. I was just about to tell David about Norman going to get Aunt Izzie when he picked up my sketch pad. It was opened to the picture of young Norman on the farm. "That one's good." He flipped through the pages. "That one, too . . . What's this?"

Before I could snatch it, David had jumped to his feet with my comic *The Gravedigger Cometh* in his hands. "*Motherless? Godless? . . . Abandoned and feared by all?* This your idea of a joke?"

"No. I mean, yes. It's just a joke. Don't get mad."

I stood up and tried to take the pad from him, but he held it out of my reach.

"This is how you pay someone back who helped you out? You draw dirt like this and share it with your little friends?"

I couldn't believe it. David's face was twisted up and his lip was puffed out. If he was a regular kind of person, I'd have said he was this close to crying.

"You listen up. You keep your yap shut and listen good. I never done nothing to you. I never done nothing to nobody. There might be some people who don't want to associate with me, but I got my brothers and I got family and my best friend, Kenny, too, down there in Lower Sackville."

"I didn't—"

"That's 'cause you never asked! I might not have a mother, but I got Dad, and he has just as good a job as your dad's. And he's *decent* and he's never laid a hand on us, not like some people's fathers. And if we don't go to church, maybe it's because there's no place for you at the church when your mother does that to herself—you ever think of that? What's your parents' excuse for staying at home every Sunday? You don't have no right—*no right*—to look down on me."

"I don't! I—"

"I don't care if you do! I'm through with you. And anyway, these are just stupid. They're stupid rip-offs of other pictures and don't mean a thing." He dropped the sketch pad to the porch and stomped back to his own house.

I sat down shakily on the step. The sun was setting behind the Flynns' house, up there above ours. For the first time since the beginning of summer, there was a little chill in the night air. I picked up my sketch pad and smoothed down the pages of my latest comic, *The Adventures of Captain Unbelievable*. And you know what? David was right. *Captain Unbelievable* was just a rip-off of *Detective Fantastic* and *Superman* and a bunch of others, anyone could see that. All my artwork was just imitations. What was that expression? A poor man's Superman. I thought for a split-sec about a hero called Poor Man, but that was so stupid I wanted to hurl myself off the porch.

How could there be any stories left in the world to tell? L. M. Montgomery was always writing about orphans who talked too much and didn't have a lot of friends, and she was probably just writing about herself and no one ever called her out for it. Imagine all those orphans on an island as big as your pinky and never running into each other. The Island of Chatterboxes. But L. M. Montgomery made every story *seem* like it was brand new. It was a good trick.

No one ever writes a comic book about a kid with a really old mother. Or a girl who loves to sing but can't make the noise coming out of her mouth match the one in her head. Or a boy whose mother let go of his hand. Or a young man who just up and left one day. Maybe I'd want to read that one. In a way, I'd been trying to read it, and I was sort of making it up as I went, too. It started in a small place, a village. A long drive away from the capital, where most things happened, like the Queen coming to visit. But this time something happened in the village, where a handsome boy lived. If a person were to write a comic book about the handsome boy, they'd probably give him the power to make himself invisible. But that wouldn't be right. What happened is, he ran off. He ran so fast, he vanished. Maybe he ran so fast, he ran around the earth. Maybe he got airborne. Maybe he was orbiting the planet right now. Maybe a person might look up and think they're seeing a distant moon or star streaking across the sky, but what they're really seeing is a flash of handsome, still running. Maybe he can't come down. I don't know. I've looked, but I've never seen a falling star.

Chapter Fourteen

It was the first time Norman didn't come into my room to say goodnight. When I fell asleep, he and Freddie hadn't even come home yet. At some point in the night, Martha crawled into my bed. I woke up with my face pressed to the back of her nightgown. She didn't stir when I slipped my feet onto the floor.

I took my sketch pad and pencils downstairs to do my morning exercises. Martha's bedroom door was shut. There was a pair of ladies' brown lace-ups at the foot of the stairs. Freddie's car was parked out front. Norman was in the kitchen reading the newspaper, his finger following the line. His knuckles were red-raw.

I opened my sketch pad to a clean page and sat there looking at it for a while. Then I pushed it away and crossed my arms on the table and rested my head on my arms, and my eyes drifted back to Norman's hands. I thought about how Johnny seemed all grown up when he was only twelve and what David had said about how him seeming bigger when I was smaller. That's what artists call perspective. How things look depends on the angle you're looking from. But there's another kind of perspective, like how Mama says that hindsight is twenty-twenty. I think that means things seem a lot clearer when they're in the past. Makes me wonder how far away you have to be from something before you can see it.

His father's been beating the tar out of him.

I raised my head. "Norman?"

"Bean."

"Where's Freddie?"

"Dropped him off last night so's we could borrow the car today."

"Did you bring back Aunt Izzie?"

"Yup."

"Why?"

"Thought it would be nice for Mama to have her sister around, seeing as how she's got a few more weeks to go with that cast."

"How did you hurt your hand?"

Norman glanced at his knuckles. "Banged it on the doorframe when I was taking out the suitcase. Your brother shouldn't let an old geezer like me do the lifting."

"Norman?"

"Hey?"

"I think you been lying to me."

Norman looked up from his paper, then folded it and set it next to his coffee cup. He reached across the table. His palm felt rough on my arm. "Oh, Bean."

"Why did you go get Aunt Izzie?"

"Well. Things have been rough for her lately."

"Because of Uncle Ezra?"

"That's right."

"And with Johnny gone off?"

"Ach," said Norman. "Course you know. I guess I should have figured, eh? I don't know why we think we can make things easier on you kids."

"You didn't tell the others, either?"

Norman shook his head. "Just your brother. A few days ago." That made me feel a little better. As better as you can feel when the worst thing possible turns out to be the stone-cold truth. "It's a hard situation. Your mother and I, we were hoping it would work itself out."

"Why didn't he tell anyone where he was going?"

Norman shook his head. "That's not for me to say. But, you know, there's a lot of people who don't have an easy time of growing up."

Like Norman himself. And David. I thought about what Norman had said about how a person's never quite right when they lose their mother so young. Mama had lost her mother young, too.

"I'd forgotten that Uncle Ezra could be rough sometimes," I said. "Mama said that Granddad could be rough after he took to the bottle, but he still had a healthy respect for God."

Norman didn't say anything for a long while. His lips were working a bit, like they were trying on different words. Finally, he said, "Your uncle has a healthy respect for the bottle."

He picked up his coffee cup and took it to the sink. "I know you want to understand better than I'm telling you, Bean, but I don't want you asking your aunt about this. It's her private business until she makes it someone else's. Do you understand?"

"Yes."

"That's my good girl. Now look, I got to check the warehouse, then I'm taking the rest of the day off. How do you like that?"

"I think that's maybe the first time you ever did."

Norman checked his watch. "Tell you what. You get yourself into some outside clothes without disturbing your sister, and I'll show you something."

Norman always worked at least a half day on Saturdays. Sometimes he drove the company truck to the warehouse to make sure everything was okay there. Today, we took Freddie's car. After he undid the padlock, Norman hauled open the big doors. He reached up into a cranny and took down a light bulb and he screwed the light bulb into the fixture hanging down over the doors.

Inside, blinking back at us, were cats, everywhere, curled up among the bags of seed and peat and fertilizer. They stretched and yawned while Norman took the lid off a barrel and pulled out a bag of food. He put the food in little cardboard crates that had been stacked beside the door.

"I thought you didn't like cats," I said. "You shoot at Mrs. Hewitt's when they get into the garden."

"These are working cats. They keep the mice down."

The cats came down from their perches and the bolder ones swirled around our legs. My heart just about broke when the kittens ventured out, with their tiny ears and tiny, pink-padded toes and tiny mews.

"Can't we take one home?" I begged when Norman had finished his rounds. I had a kitten in each hand, their tiny hearts beating against my palms.

"Why do you think I never bring you down here?" Norman chuckled. "You know they'll make your sister's asthma worse."

"We can't just leave them."

"You see any dead cats? It's not like we force 'em to live here. But you can choose one for your friend."

"Who? . . . David?"

I guess it was clear enough from my face that David and I'd had another fight.

"Pick a good mouser. And then you take it over to him and see if that don't smooth things over."

I surveyed the kittens. Three of them tumbled around together by the food barrel. Another slept on an empty burlap sack, and a little tabby leaned against Norman's shoe. Then I spied a black-and-white one pouncing on a hose. I picked him up, and when I went to snuggle him, he batted my glasses with his feet.

"You're our boy." I laughed. "Like to see you take on a Flynn, though."

I took him out to Freddie's car while Norman put the food crates away. Just before he unscrewed the light bulb, he reached down and scooped up the little tabby that had followed him to the door.

"People need a little company in this world," he said, reaching through the car window to put the tabby next to the scrapper on my lap.

Which is true enough. Even though, strictly speaking, cats aren't people.

After we got home we left the kittens in the car until I could find a basket or something to put them in. Soon as we passed between the front hedges, we could hear Mama and Martha inside. Laughing. We followed the sound into the kitchen, where Martha had her head down on the table, shoulders shaking, and Mama's face was buried in her apron. Aunt Izzie was pouring tea with one hand and wiping her eyes with the other. She was the same height as Mama, but where Mama's hair was white, Aunt Izzie's was steel-grey. Her skin was darker and she had the same brown eyes as the rest of us and she was heavy and sturdy but softer-looking than Mama. And when she came over and put her arms around me, she had a smell that was half spice, half flowers.

"It's like looking in a mirror!" she said when she saw me. "A mirror that's forty years old!" She laughed a raspy laugh that yanked the corners of my mouth in all directions. "Look at you! Grown up!" She spun me round and hugged me tight. "Norman, this can't be your Bean."

"I should have been calling her Sprout, eh?"

"Hewo," I muffled into Aunt Izzie's housedress, my glasses smushed into my face.

When I was able to look at her again, I saw that her eyes were leaking tears. "I get from A to Zed so fast these days," she said, wiping her face again.

"Good Lord, she's not a piece of dough," Mama scolded as

128

Aunt Izzie turned me around for the fifth time. "Stop manhandling the poor girl."

"We're old hens, Lily. You can't boss your baby sister," Aunt Izzie said. "All right, fine. Norman, we'd better get to those errands. We got to prepare for a certain someone's birthday tomorrow, and no one's going to neglect the youngest's big day on my watch. Now that I'm here to keep your mother from serving her vanilla cake, it'll be a real party!"

The stone walk leading up to the Flynns' house had little bits of clover growing in the cracks. As I got closer—as slowly as I could manage without taking any backwards steps—I saw the white paint around the front windows was chipping. Underneath were cheerful pink, red, and orange flowers planted in tidy rows.

David opened the door before I even knocked.

"What are you doing here?"

"That's not very polite," I said.

"Oh. It's just you never come over before."

I pulled back the towel covering the old milk crate I was carrying and thrust the crate towards him. "I heard you like kittens for breakfast."

The moment I said it, I caught a whiff of something sweet— wild strawberries, maybe—carried on the breeze.

That made me think of jam.

And jam made me think of the jelly cupboard inside the Flynn house.

And the jelly cupboard made me think of how really dumb Marcy could be sometimes.

"You got cats? That's a bad joke."

"I know. Sorry. I'm sorry," I said. "They're for you. The Nelson Seed warehouse is full of them and Norman was thinking you could use a good mouser. Or two. What's the matter? You don't like cats?"

"No. I mean, I like them fine. I'll have to ask my dad if it's okay."

"Okay."

David took the milk crate from me and stepped out of the house, closing the door behind him. "It's not too clean in there," he said. "You need a woman for that, I guess. There's just my Aunt Eileen, sometimes, when she comes up from the Valley."

We sat down on the stoop. David's neck was flushed where his hair curled above his shirt collar. He put his hand in the crate to scratch the little tabby under her chin. She closed her eyes and purred. The little scrapper was trying to chew off David's cuff.

"That one's Flynn," I said. "Haven't named the other one."

"Flynn Flynn?"

And just like that, the fight was broken.

I told David about Aunt Izzie arriving in the night and what Norman had told me that morning. "Strange about Martha walking by the shipyard, then," I said. "I wonder what she was doing down there."

"You'll have to ask her," David said. "Where do you think Norman's taking your aunt?"

"Errands, I think."

"Anywhere else?"

"Where else?"

"Think about it. Did Norman tell you he didn't know where Johnny is?"

I whacked David on his knee. "You think Norman's taking Aunt Izzie down to the shipyard? You think they're gonna see Johnny?"

"Dunno. Gotta wonder, though."

"What should we do? Should we—let's go down there!"

"Hold up, hold up. I told your dad I'd stack firewood today and I'm gonna. Besides, maybe what he's thinking is they're going to bring your cousin back."

"For my birthday!"

"It's your birthday?"

Sometimes a person can pour a big bucket of shame over her head all by herself. I never thought to invite David to my birthday dinner.

"It's tomorrow."

"That's it then. But I suppose they gotta wrap him up first.

131

Put a little bow on his perfect little head. Or what did you call it? His dark-black-night-dark hair?"

"Hey!"

"Hey, yourself. I got firewood to get to."

David stomped down the steps, flattening the clover, the kittens bouncing inside the milk crate tucked under his arm.

"Just shows!" I yelled. "You can take the Gravedigger out of the cemetery, but you can't take the grave . . . or the, the . . ."

I took my time walking back to the house.

Chapter Fifteen

As soon as I walked in the door, the phone rang.

"Hello?"

"Who's this?"

"Hi, Uncle Jim."

"Aw, geez. It's the kid."

"Hey, Izzie's here!"

"*Aunt* Izzie, kid. Don't be cheeky, as the aunties used to say. Rotten old bags."

"*Aunt* Izzie's here. But she's out with Norman doing birthday shopping."

"For whose birthday?"

"Mine!"

"When is it?"

"*Tomorrow.* Aunt Izzie said she wouldn't let the youngest go without a proper birthday."

"For the love of Pete. The woman has one foot in the grave and she's still going on about that youngest nonsense. Tell me, kid. How many people do you share a room with?"

"None."

"And how many jobs you got?"

"None. But I do chores."

"And which dead relative are you named after? 'Cause every other bloody member of your family is named for some old fool, first and second. Margaret Mavis. Doris Irma. Cripes."

"I don't know. Who am I named for?"

"No one. That's my point."

"So where'd 'Rosalie' come from?"

"Since your mother had fulfilled her obligations to dear sainted aunts and in-laws by the time you came along, you got named after her favourite flower. Which is ironic, when you think about it."

"What do you mean?"

"Her name's Lily. Pay attention, kid."

"Oh." I wasn't sure what 'ironic' meant.

"Listen," Uncle Jim said, "I'd love to keep pouring my life savings into this conversation, but I'd better call back when your aunt is there."

"I know why you're calling," I said. "It's about Johnny.

About him being missing. I know it."

"You do, eh? Not much to know."

"I know. Uncle Jim?"

"What?"

"Did Mama just like the name Evelyn, too? You know, 'Rosalie Evelyn'?"

"Naw, kid. Evelyn was our baby sister. Who died with our mother. You ask your Mama about that some time. She'll tell you if you ask."

Well, I didn't get a chance. Because the first thing Mama said to me when I went into the kitchen was, "Go to Jack Newberry's and get me two pounds of ground steak. Tell him if he sends you home with something fatty, it will be trotted right back to him."

"Aw geez, Mama."

"I hope that's Jesus you're calling on and not backtalk."

"Yeah, Jesus."

"Rosalie Evelyn . . ."

"I'm going."

I took the money. Rain clouds were gathering, the excitement of Aunt Izzie's visit was wearing off fast, and who knew how long it would be before Norman and Izzie came back with Johnny? I let the screen door bang shut behind me.

"Looks like someone's having a bad day."

His dark hair was wild-looking, like he'd been riding with the car windows open. He'd grown a moustache since I'd last saw him, and his breath came hard through his nose. I'll tell you something about perspective, though. Standing there, at the end of our walk, Uncle Ezra was bigger than I remembered.

"Been a while. You recognize me, Rosalie?" He had a small parcel under his arm.

"Yes, sir."

"Your folks home?"

"Just Mama. And Martha."

"In the kitchen, you think?"

I nodded.

David came around the corner of the house just as Uncle Ezra went in. "That him? Johnny?"

"Oh, no! That's . . ." I couldn't make my words work. "That's his father."

"Let's go inside."

David put his hand on my back and pushed me gently.

Mama and Martha were sitting at the kitchen table and Uncle Ezra was pacing the floor. "Who's this?" he said, when David and I appeared in the doorway.

"The hired help," said David. His chin jutted out and he folded his arms.

"This is family business."

"I don't mind."

Uncle Ezra held David's hard stare for a moment, then took the parcel from under his arm and placed it on the table. Nobody moved.

"Not curious? Here, have a look," he said to me.

I hesitated. "Go on," whispered David.

I walked over to the table. The Kellocks' address in Ship Harbour was written out in black marker on the rumpled brown paper. No return address. I undid the string that was loosely tied around the package, peeled back the paper, and opened the cardboard box.

Inside, there were some official-looking papers. A thin wallet. A pocket comb. A couple of old comic books. A wristwatch with a dirty leather strap. A birth certificate. For William John Kellock. A note, also written in black marker, on lined paper torn from a scribbler. It read, in block letters:

JOHNNY KELLOCK DIED TODAY.

On every carnival ride I ever took, no matter how much I begged to get on, there came a point when I'd do just about anything to get off. I had that feeling now, plus a whole other kind of panic, like I was the one who'd put this in motion and I couldn't stop it.

A hush had fallen over the odd jumble of things on Mama's

table. All that was left of Johnny. The letters on the paper I held seemed to blur together and reshape themselves into new words, fearsome words, wicked words:

SOMEONE ELSE FOUND HIM FIRST.

"What do you think about that?" Uncle Ezra said to Mama, leaning on the table.

"I heard about it already from Izzie."

"Doesn't that break you up, knowing your nephew is departed?"

"I know what you been saying about this."

"Did she tell you he took two thousand dollars from the station's safe?"

"No."

"Two thousand dollars. The last of the money from selling your father's place. That cleans us out."

"I'm thinking there used to be a lot more than two thousand dollars, but someone's been drinking it away."

"I haven't had a drop since the day he left."

But you could smell the liquor on him now.

"I know you don't have much in the bank," Mama said, "where your savings should have been."

"You also know I like to be able to put my hands on my money, same as your husband. Only I can't because my boy made off with it," said Uncle Ezra. "You notice there's nothing in that box about no bank accounts. Or do you figure he spent everything already? Died shopping?"

Martha rose from her chair. She had a look. If I had to sum it up in one word I'd say it was "No!" She walked unsteadily over to the coat hooks, put on her hat, and went out the back door, closing it softly behind her.

"There's no death certificate, either," said Mama.

"He'll turn up when the money runs out."

"A person doesn't go to this kind of trouble if they're expecting to come back. Now, I think you'd better be off. Norman's on his way," Mama said. "I don't know if you want another run-in with him."

I wished it were true. What I wouldn't have given to hear Norman's lunch pail hitting the hall table.

Uncle Ezra pointed his finger at Mama and said, real quiet-like, "Someone knows where my son is." He began to pace a little. "Norman find him work? Get him boarded somewhere? Maybe he's with Jim, hey? That where he is?"

Mama sighed. "You can't keep track of your own son, don't you be blaming me. I raised enough kids already."

"Tell me where he is!"

You could feel the heat coming off him. Lord, what it must be to live in that man's house, like living with the devil himself.

"Rosalie, David," Mama said. "You better get to that firewood."

"But Mama—"

"Before it gets damp. Go."

But Ezra was between me and the door and he grabbed me by the arm. "Hey!" Before I had even realized what Ezra intended, David was running towards us with his head like a battering ram, and just as quick was sent skidding across the floor. He was soon back on his feet and shook out his head, but Mama had raised herself up and she put her hand on his shoulder. You could see in his mind he was straining like a dog on a leash.

"You never showed no respect for no one," Ezra said to Mama. "Not even your father."

"Men who hurt children," said Mama, " . . . are not men."

Those sausage-y fingers were digging into my arm. "Where's my son?" he said, and then he was wailing. "Where's my son? Where's my son?" It was the biggest, saddest, scariest sound I ever heard in my life.

Uncle Ezra's hand encircled my rib cage. He squeezed the air right out of me as he dragged me across the kitchen. It was like the time I jumped into a cold lake 'cause Marcy dared me and I when I came up I was gasping like a fish on the bottom of a boat. Ezra's other hand, the one clutching my arm, moved down to my wrist and reached towards the bubbling chowder on the stove. Then I heard a note, like the opening trill of a hymn, like a whole choir coming off a hallelujah, and holy God it was me. The air came flooding back into my lungs just before my hand touched that hot broth, and I squeezed my eyes shut and screamed, "I know where Johnny is!"

When I opened my eyes, David's face was stopped right there in front of mine. His dark curls trembled on his forehead and he gripped my hand above where Ezra had me at the wrist. "Johnny's with Norman and Izzie," I said, my breath on David's face. "Down at the shipyard."

Ezra let go. He pushed past David and me, and the over-turned chairs that David had knocked over when he lunged across the kitchen, and Mama, caught behind the chairs with Norman's big black umbrella frozen in the air.

David went after him. I don't know what he was planning— there was no way he was going to be able to stop Ezra—but I don't figure he was thinking ahead, and neither was I when I followed. Sometimes a person's feet just take over. We made it to the screen door to see Ezra backing back up the porch steps. Norman pounded the front walk towards him. Aunt Izzie stood on the lawn, holding a large cake box in front of her like a shield.

In all my life, I'm never going to see anything like it again: Norman taking the steps two at a time, grabbing hold of Uncle Ezra, and throwing him off the porch, almost clear of the yard, as though he was tossing a bale of hay or a sack of seed, like he done a million times since he was twelve years old. One heave and Ezra hit the end of the walk and rolled onto the street.

I'm glad to say that Norman didn't kill my uncle—that he didn't have to. Because when Ezra got over the shock of being tossed and scraped on the hot cement, he slowly got himself up and into his car and drove away.

And that's how Aunt Izzie came to stay with us for good.

Chapter Sixteen

Aunt Izzie sat on the chesterfield beside Mama, Norman's cigar box open on her lap. She was reading the letter that she had pulled out from under the bundle of money. I couldn't make out the words from the landing, where David and I were sitting, but by now I recognized the neat, loopy handwriting.

"I thought he'd stolen it," Aunt Izzie said, when she'd finished the letter.

"No," said Norman. "Just sent it here for safekeeping. By post. I near had a heart attack when I saw that. It even went to the wrong house. But we got it back." He winked at me. "I been protecting it."

Aunt Izzie looked down at the flimsy old cigar box.

"Norman won't be happy until we're robbed blind," said

Mama. "He's probably got rubies in the toes of those socks he's wearing."

Tears slid down Aunt Izzie's cheeks. "Johnny's not coming back. This is planned out. He said he'd do what he had to, but I never expected him to go this far."

"Hush that. Anyway, I should have said about the money," said Norman. "It only came just before you told us he'd gone off. You found it, didn't you, Lily? I was hoping not to add to your worries."

Mama shrugged.

"Never could keep a secret from you."

"He asked you to keep it safe until I left and you did," said Aunt Izzie. "I suppose we were all hoping he'd make his way here."

"But he is here, isn't he?" I said. "Didn't you go down to the shipyard to see him, Norman?"

"Where are you getting this?" Mama asked.

"Gerry Flynn. He said there's a new guy named John who works there."

If you saw the look I got from David in a comic book, you wouldn't need a bubble to tell you what he was thinking:

There's a hole in the backyard with your name on it.

"He was probably talking about young John Hubley, Ray Campbell's nephew," said Norman.

"Oh."

144

"I went down to speak to Mr. Flynn about getting David a new job at Nelson Seed. Didn't want to ask in front of the boy."

David's cheeks flushed. "Thank you, sir," he said. "I sure would like that."

Norman smiled. "You could come down to talk to the boss man next week."

"Johnny would have liked a job at the shipyard," said Aunt Izzie. "But he bought a ticket to Montreal instead. Or maybe Toronto. Someone told me they thought they saw him at the train station."

We had got it all wrong. Start to finish. Mama hadn't lied about the envelope that came from Ship Harbour; Norman hadn't showed it to her. Martha found the money Johnny sent, not Norman's savings, and she must have been crying over the letter that came with it, not because we might move. It was a different John that got work at the shipyard, just like it was a different Jimmy who drowned that day in Friar's Lake, when Mama thought Marshall Briggsby was going on about my Uncle Jim. Some stranger knew better than anyone else where Johnny was, and none of us knew if he was ever coming home.

"You kids have been barking up the wrong tree," Aunt Izzie said, like she'd used X-ray vision on my brain. That was one of Judge Haliburton's expressions. Here's another one: *Facts are stranger than fiction.*

The screen door creaked.

When I saw the shadow behind Martha, it was as if, for one second, someone had pulled the brake on the carnival ride. We were all suspended there, at the top of a gigantic wheel, looking over everything that had happened. And down below, making their way through the crowds of tiny people, were Martha and Johnny.

Then they stepped into the room and he took off his cap.

It was Gerry Flynn.

"We were watching from across the way. Mr. Norman sure gave that guy the old heave-ho," he said. "I met up with this one as she was leaving the house"—he nodded at Martha— "and I says to myself, she looks pretty darn upset, maybe I'll say something, and then I think, nah, mind your own business, Gerry, you never hardly said two words to each other before, but then I'm saying hello, we get to talking and stuff, and then we seen what happened and . . . here we are."

"I guess we should shove off," David said, standing up.

Norman shook David's hand, then went over and shook Gerry's.

Through the screen door, I watched David pick up the kittens, which had been stalking each other on the porch, and put them back in the milk crate. He followed his brother down the steps, across the street, and up the steps into their own house. It was like he was boarding a ship or something. And our house was a different ship. And Agricola Street was a plank between us.

There was a faintly boozy smell coming from Martha.

"Johnny's not dead," said Mama. "You hear me? That was just some foolish trick to stop people from looking for him. He's only . . ."

She felt around for the right word.

"Disappeared," I said.

Martha sat down on the chesterfield next to Aunt Izzie, who squeezed her close. "We made a promise, a long time ago, that we would try to go to the same university," said Martha. "Just had to hang in there." She looked up at Mama. "I don't mean I ever minded . . ." Mama cut her off with a wave of her hand. " . . . I didn't expect to hold him to it, not really, but I always thought he'd make his way back to the city one day."

"You know," said Aunt Izzie, "your Uncle Jim was forever running off from the aunties."

"But then one time he didn't come back," said Martha. "He went to work at the farm."

"And if he hadn't," Mama said, "he wouldn't have met Norman and Ezra, and you wouldn't be sitting here today and Johnny wouldn't be sitting wherever he is, God bless him. Sometimes people have to go off and sort things out for themselves."

"Some of us take a little longer to get going," said Aunt Izzie. "Which is how they end up having babies at near fifty years old!"

Mama gave Aunt Izzie a pinch in her side and for a moment they didn't look like a couple of old hens. They looked like the little girls in the photographs.

Martha eventually fessed up to my parents that she'd found out about Johnny from snooping to see how much money Norman had saved. And Norman fessed up that if there'd been more room in the cigar box, she would have also found his winnings from the baseball pool and selling Irish Sweepstakes tickets on the side, and Mama said, "You did not say that and I did not hear that."

Norman said, "Nope."

No one ever asked me how I knew Johnny had gone off. Maybe they figured I'd overheard something, which was true in a roundabout kind of way. Or maybe it just didn't matter any more. Maybe it was just easier to take an eraser to things and start over.

Aunt Izzie sure wasn't one to keep things to herself. "Whew. Dropped a rose," she'd announce as she walked into a room, and the eggy smell would follow. Or she'd smile sweetly at Mama and say, "Don't Lil's rump look just like a popover in that housedress?" She wouldn't let up until Martha and me were gripping our stomachs.

In time, I heard about Aunt Izzie waking up to find Johnny's bed made and his suitcase missing. No note or anything, just a memory of him saying that he never wanted to see Uncle Ezra lay a hand on another person ever again. Aunt Izzie said she wouldn't have left so long as Johnny was there, and Johnny wouldn't leave so long as she stayed.

Until he did. And when she still didn't leave, because she kept thinking he'd come back, well, maybe that's when Johnny decided he was gone for good. But, as I said back at the start, we might never know for certain.

"That's what letting your kids read too many comics does," said Aunt Izzie. "Makes them right dramatic."

There was a warm breeze with a little ripple of cool under it as Martha, Aunt Izzie, and I headed off to church on my birthday. A bit of autumn slipping into the summer air. I held my head high as we went by the caterwauler in her pew, and I didn't mouth the words to the hymn. You could hardly hear me over Aunt Izzie, anyway. She sounded like a cat filled with air and whacked against a shed, and I can't describe it any better than that.

The family came over for Sunday dinner. Doris's stomach, full of the baby that was almost due, got in the door about three minutes before the rest of her. My nephew, Bennie, and my niece, Laura, came with Margaret and Cecil. They had grown up a lot over the summer, but they still trailed me everywhere like little ducks. No one made an announcement about why Aunt Izzie was there or what was going on with Johnny. But I could tell the news was making its way through the family. People went to her in ones and twos, and you'd see them chatting quietly, with a hand on her arm or around her shoulder.

After I blew out the candles on the store-bought cherry-swirl cake, us Normans ended up around Mama's kitchen table in the usual order—oldest to youngest—Freddie, Margaret, Doris, Young Lil, Martha, and me. With everyone else squeezed in between. There was talk of Norman going out Prospect way to have a look at that nice property, after all. We argued—like we had any say-so—about whether we should move and how much we'd get for the Agricola Street house, and what kind of car we'd buy so Norman could drive to his job in the city. I knew that if we left the North End, Mama's table would come with us, but it wouldn't be the same. It was already not quite the same. We hardly fit around it. And I wondered how many more times we'd all sit together like that.

It wasn't long before my sisters lit up. Martha kept her hand near the inhaler in her pocket like a cowboy waiting for the "Draw!" Young Lil pushed her pack of cigarettes towards me. I pulled one out of the foil wrapper and held it between my lips. It had a musty taste to it. She showed me how to suck in while she held her lighter to the end. Everyone waited for me to choke—but I didn't.

"Oh, hell," Mama said. "Like a fish to water."

I smiled and took a deep drag. Then, my throat filled with smoke, I said, "Fetch some ground steak. If Jack Newberry sends you home with something fatty, it will be trotted right back to him."

I tell you, I had them hooting and pounding the table.

Mama said, "Very funny, smarty-pants. Now go upstairs and fetch my—"

"Noxema!" Everyone laughed.

"I'm ashamed of all of you."

The truth is I was glad for the chance to mush the cigarette into the ashtray.

From Mama and Norman's bedroom window, I could see my niece, Laura, pushing her brother on the swing. It was there when I came down that morning, like it had sprouted from the tree branch in the night. The ropes were old, but the seat had been painted the girliest pink you ever saw, and it was wrapped with a wide red ribbon. It hung from the old maple like a promise.

Rrrrrring!

"How do you know?" I yelled at the blue frog. But this time, instead of running, I slapped my hand down on the receiver, brought it to my ear, and cleared my throat.

"Aunt Lily? Got your message."

If I'd had my wits about me, I might have tried to pull it off. I might have pretended I was Mama, or just told him straight out that we were hoping he'd come home soon, that his mother was here and it looked like she was going to stay on. Maybe he already knew. Maybe Mama had told him on her upstairs telephone. But Johnny realized he'd made a mistake and before I could say anything, he hung up.

You probably never heard that my Mama has more pages than a hymn book. Each one is so thin you might look right through it and not see what's written there. But the words are there, layers and layers of them, even if they are old and hard to understand.

I went downstairs and put the Noxema jar on the table in front of Mama. Then I wrapped my arms around her shoulders and pressed my face to her wrinkled cheek. "I'm sorry I hurt your ankle," I said.

And suddenly, even though my mind was filled up with Johnny, and how Mama had kept his secret all this time, and how she would keep it, no matter what, because that was the thing about Mama, it came to me about the next picture I was going to draw.

Mama squeezed my arm. "Spilt milk," she said.

Still, she didn't let go.

Acknowledgements

I have borrowed, here and there, real places and historic events and turned them into fiction. But that does not make this a true story.

There was a Johnny Kellock who went looking for a better life. I hope he found it.

I owe a special thank you to my mother, Rose, for sharing her name and her memories. Thanks, too, to those who helped me shape this story into a book, especially Lena Coakley, Kathy Stinson, Paula Wing, the Eisan family, and my editor, Lynne Missen.